TARANTULAS ON THE BRAIN

About the Author

Marilyn Singer is the author of a number of novels and picture books. She lives with her husband, Steven Aronson, in a Brooklyn brownstone with three dogs, pigeons, chinchillas and a parakeet, but no tarantula. She once took care of her neighbor's tarantula—Elizabeth R.—who was the inspiration for this book.

**Other APPLE PAPERBACKS®
you will enjoy:**

TARANTULAS ON THE BRAIN

Marilyn Singer

Illustrated by
Leigh Grant

AN
APPLE®
PAPERBACK

SCHOLASTIC INC.
New York Toronto London Auckland Sydney Tokyo

Acknowledgements
Thanks to Bill Aronson for his tips on prestidigitation
and to Steve Aronson for his title and his willing ears.

ISBN 0-590-33103-5

12 11 10 9 8 7 6 5 4 3 2 1   9   4 5 6 7 8/8
Printed in the U.S.A.   11

To Andrew Ottiger

tarantula (tə ran′ chə lə), *n.*, *pl.* **-las, -lae** (-lē′).
1. any of several large, hairy spiders of the family
Theraphosidae, as *Dugesiella hentzi*, of the south-
western U.S., having a painful but not highly venom-
ous bite. . . .

Aunt Minnie is always telling me the story of the
ugly duckling. You know the one—it's about this
funny-looking duckling that everyone laughs at and
then it has the last laugh because it grows up to be
a big, beautiful swan. The reason she keeps telling
me this story is because *I'm* pretty funny-looking—
I've got long legs and humongous feet, and buck teeth,
too—and Aunt Minnie hopes *I'll* grow up and become
a swan. But I keep telling her I don't want to be a

swan because swans are nasty, mean birds that can break your leg with one swat of a wing if they want to. You see, people are always misjudging animals because of their looks. Take spiders, for instance. Especially tarantulas. People look at tarantulas and see their long, hairy legs and their fat, fuzzy bodies and they scream and yell and say how horrible tarantulas are. But they don't understand tarantulas at all. Tarantulas are soft and gentle and they never bite—well, almost never—unless they're attacked first. I'd rather become a tarantula than a swan any day. I told Mom and Dad that, but they said, "Oh Lizzie, honestly!" They're just as bad as everybody else.

But my sister Rona is even worse. She says the only thing spiders are good for is to be stepped on, and that only a brat could like them. "Lizzie, you're a brat," she says.

Once, I asked her why she thinks I'm a brat, but she just said, "Well, if you don't know, I won't bother to tell you."

"That's a very unscientific answer," I said.

"You and your science! Science won't get you a boyfriend," she sneered.

I told her she'd make a good black widow spider when she grows up.

Then she got real mad and said a remark like that proved I was a brat and she stomped off to call her friend Judy and talk about boys.

I think if Rona spent more time studying science than looking in the mirror to see if her breasts are growing, she'd know a lot more about life and spiders. And maybe even boys.

I got interested in spiders when we rented a house in Vermont last summer. Mom was punishing me for leaving a hot dog and a hamburger under my bed. I guess I should explain. See, I've been interested in scientific experiments for a long time. I was trying to find out if mold grew faster on a hot dog or on a burger. I never did find out, because two days after I put them under my bed, Mom found them. Boy, was she mad.

"Lizzie," she said, "leaving meat under your bed would be bad enough in your own house, but in someone else's house it's disgusting."

I tried to explain that it was an experiment, but Mom said she didn't want to hear about it, and she made me stay home while she and Dad and Rona went swimming.

I stood on the porch and watched them go. I was feeling kind of sad. I sat down trying to figure out what to do, when right in front of my face I saw this beautiful orb spider in her beautiful web. Of course, I didn't know it was an orb spider then. But I did know it was beautiful. I just sat and watched it for ages. It seemed to know just what it was doing.

When Mom and Dad and Rona came back, I had

forgotten I was sad. I had even forgotten I was being punished, and I asked Mom if we could go to the library and get out a book on spiders.

Rona threw me one of her "Oh brother" looks, and Mom reminded me I was still being punished, so I didn't get to find out it was an orb spider until the next day. I've been interested in spiders ever since. But especially in tarantulas, because they're so neat and so misunderstood.

My best friend, Tessa, says there's nothing bratty about liking spiders. Tessa likes them very much and nobody could ever call her a brat. She's eleven, a year older than me, and she's got big, blue eyes and long, curly blond hair. She wears lots of pretty dresses with tucks or ribbons or something her mother calls "ruching" on them. She also does real well in everything at school. Not like me. The only thing I do well in is science. Tessa has a pet iguana whose name is Verde, which means "green" in Spanish and which is a good name for him because he's the greenest green lizard you ever saw.

I don't have any pets, because Mom says she's allergic to animals. "Not to spiders?" I asked.

"Especially to spiders," she said.

But I think she was joking.

Tessa and I met after I ate Julie Lindstrom's tuna-fish-and-cheese sandwich. I ate it because Tommy Fredericks sat down and squished my peanut-butter-

and-banana sandwich and I was really hungry that day. Julie whined and yowled and told the teacher I stole her sandwich, so I got sent to the older kids' cooking class to make her another one, and there was Tessa. She helped me make a cream-cheese-and-olives sandwich, but Julie Lindstrom said it was yucky and wouldn't eat it. Anyway, Tessa and I liked each other right away, and were surprised and happy to find out we live only two blocks apart. She brought me home to meet Verde and told me all about him and other lizards. Tessa's mother liked me too. She still does even though I nearly scared her to death yesterday at The American Museum of Natural History, where I made my big decision.

The Museum of Natural History is a very scientific place where there are lots of lizards and spiders and other animals. Except that all of the animals are stuffed. I asked Tessa how you stuff an animal and she said she wasn't sure, but she'd look it up.

The animals that aren't stuffed are skeletons. They've got horse skeletons thousands and thousands of years old. Boy, horses were really little then. Smaller than Great Danes. I wanted to ask the guard if I could try sitting on one to see if it would hold me up, but Ms. Lawrence said she didn't think the museum would appreciate it. It was after the horse skeletons I got lost and nearly scared Ms. Lawrence to death. Well, not really lost. I knew where I was, but

Tessa and Ms. Lawrence didn't. They went off to see the Neanderthal man and I was following along, but on the way I saw a sign that said: INSECTS AND SPIDERS.

"Here it is! Let's go look!" I called, but I guess they didn't hear me.

I walked into this room with all these cases full of bugs and spiders and things. They're all dead, of course, but real lifelike. There were beetles almost as big as my hand and scorpions with the stingers curled up looking ready to strike and beautiful bird-wing butterflies in a zillion colors. And then I saw them. The tarantulas. There were even more kinds than I thought there were. Some were gigantic; others weren't so big. Some were sort of dull brown, but my favorite was black and orange and looked just like velvet. I never saw a real one before—just photographs—and I couldn't take my eyes off it; I just stood there looking and looking until Tessa and Ms. Lawrence and two guards came in all talking loud together: "There she is, miss." "Oh, Lizzie, I knew you'd be here." "Are you okay, little girl?" "Lizzie, how could you just disappear like that? You nearly scared me to death!"

After that, Ms. Lawrence took us both to the cafeteria to have lunch, but I knew it was to make sure I didn't disappear again.

"Tessa," I whispered when we were standing on line, "I saw the tarantulas."

"I know." Tessa nodded.

"Tessa, I just have to have one. A live one. Even if I have to sneak it into my room and hide it from Mom."

Tessa nodded again.

"Will you help me?"

"Sure."

"Is this a private conference or can anyone attend?" Ms. Lawrence said.

I jumped.

"We're just trying to decide what to eat, Mom," Tessa answered quickly.

Ms. Lawrence looked at her like she knew better, but she didn't say anything.

I smiled at Tessa and, when her mother wasn't looking, linked my pinkie in hers. That's our special signal. It means, "You're on."

Tomorrow we execute Step A of our plan: Find the Tarantula.

2

"Hello. Fin and Feather Pet Shop? I'm interested in acquiring a pet tarantula. Do you have any for sale? No? Okay. Thank you." Tessa hung up the phone. "Struck out again," she said. "With all the pet shops in Brooklyn, you'd think someone would have a tarantula."

"Looks like we'll have to try Manhattan." I sighed.

"We don't have a Manhattan yellow pages," Tessa said.

"There's one at the library. We can copy down the phone numbers there." Then I thought of something—"Hey, didn't you get Verde in Manhattan?"

"No. New Jersey. Near where I used to live."

"Did they have tarantulas at that shop?"

"Yeah. Big ones. I remember because they were

noisy. I mean, I thought they were noisy, but it turned out to be the crickets they were going to eat."

"New Jersey's too far. I guess we better go to the library and get those numbers."

The library is on the next block. We ran there, copied down a whole bunch of numbers and ran back to Tessa's building.

"Let me try this time." I grabbed the phone and dialed the first number. Then I carefully held my nose.

"Why are you holding your nose?" Tessa asked.

"So no one will recognize my voice. . . . Oh, hello. Do you have any pet tarantulas for sale? What's a tarantula? Isn't this ABC Pet Shop? Oh, sorry."

Tessa had her hand over her mouth trying not to giggle.

"Anybody can get a wrong number," I said.

"What was it?"

"Ferrante's Funeral Parlor."

Tessa really cracked up. So did I.

When we stopped laughing, Tessa said, "My turn."

"No. That last one didn't count," I said.

"Oh, all right."

I tried the next number: Abie's Pets. No answer.

"Maybe Abie's in Mexico hunting for tarantulas," Tessa said.

"Mexico! Oh no!" I shouted.

"What's wrong?"

"My report for Ms. Eggleston, that's what!" I yelled.

Ms. Eggleston is my fifth-grade teacher. She's making the whole class do reports on foreign countries. I raised my hand and asked if we could do reports on interesting animals instead, but she said not for social studies. Who wants to do a report on some dumb country? My mom suggested I write about France because the food is so good. Dad said some country nobody knows much about like Yemen or Andorra would be neat. And Rona told me to do Denmark because she heard the kids are so well behaved there. But I'm not interested in those places. I finally decided I'd do Mexico because that's where tarantulas and lizards come from. But my report's due tomorrow and I haven't even started it yet.

"Oh, Lizzie, you better go write it now or Eggleston'll flunk you," Tessa said.

I sighed. "Let me try one more number. And then I'll go do my report." I looked at my list and decided to pick out the best name on it. "The Beautiful Beast? No, sounds like a beauty salon for dogs. Fat Cats? No. The Fifth Street Aquarium? No. Ah-ha! Got it! Noah's Ark!"

"Are they supposed to have two of everything?"

"I don't care—as long as they have *one* tarantula." I dialed real fast.

"Hello. Noah's Ark. We carry all God's creatures— great and small," a deep voice answered. I bet the real Noah sounded just like that.

"Oh, that's good," I said. "The creature I'm interested in is great and small. It's an arachnid—a spider. Do you have any spiders?"

"Yes, we have several kinds. What are you interested in?"

"Tarantulas. Do you have any?"

"As a matter of fact, we just received a shipment today."

"Of how many?"

"Three."

"Three!" I yelled, forgetting to hold my nose. "Are they black and orange?"

"One is. The others are brown and . . ."

"Could you save the black-and-orange one for me?"

"Not without a deposit, I'm afraid. Could you come here tomorrow—we're just closing up now—or Friday?"

"Uh. Uh. Just a minute." I put my hand over the phone. "Tessa, he wants me to come there tomorrow or Friday."

"Where is it?"

"Where is it? I'll ask. . . . Hello, where is your store?"

"On Canal Street."

I put my hand over the phone again. "Canal Street, wherever that is."

"How are we going to get there? It can't be your mother or my mother."

Step B. I had thought of the answer, but I wasn't sure Tessa would like it. "Buster," I said.

"Oh no, not Buster."

"Oh please, Tessa, just this once. You know how he loves to take you places."

Tessa put on her long-suffering face. "Lizzie, if you weren't my best friend . . ."

"Thanks, Tessa." I uncovered the phone. "Hello? We—I mean—I can come on Friday after sch—I mean Friday afternoon. Is that okay?"

But Noah had hung up.

"Oh well, he probably got tired. Oh, Tessa, Tessa, Tessa," I sang, "I'm going to get my tarantula."

"How much does it cost? How will you get it home? Where will you hide it? What will you feed it?" Tessa ticked off the questions on her fingers.

I stared at her. I hadn't thought about any of those things.

"Well, you asked me to help," she said.

"Oh, Tessa, we have to figure out the rest of the plan."

"Yes. But not now. You have to write your report."

"When then?"

"Tomorrow. Now go to the library and I'll call Buster." She made a face.

"Tessa, you're a good friend." We linked pinkies and I ran out the door.

3

"Twenty-five dollars! Where am I going to get twenty-five dollars?"

"And don't forget eighteen dollars for the tank, a dollar twenty-five for the gravel and two dollars every month for the crickets. That's forty—"

"I know, I know. Forty-six dollars and twenty-five cents plus monthly cricket costs. Oh Tessa, all I have is five dollars and fifty-seven cents."

"Maybe you could catch the crickets."

"Don't joke. What am I going to do?"

"Well, Noah said he'd take a deposit."

"Yes, five dollars. But that'll only hold her a short time. Probably only two weeks."

"How do you know it's a her?" She was grinning.

"Tessa!"

She wiped off her smile. "Okay. Then you'll have to find a way to beg, borrow, steal or earn forty dollars and sixty-eight cents in two weeks."

"How'd you figure that out so fast?"

"I'm a genius."

I blew her a raspberry.

"Ooh, you got spit on me!"

"Sorry."

We were sitting in Tessa's room on Thursday afternoon. Spread out in front of us was a sheet of paper that looked like this:

ARACHNID PLAN

Step	Problem	Solution
A	Find tarantula	Noah's Ark
B	Get to Noah's Ark	Buster
C		

Tessa was holding another sheet. On it were questions: How much does t. cost? How can L. get it home? What will L. feed it? Where will L. hide it?

"Why did you call me L.?" I asked.

"That's what they always write on charts," she said. Then she said that every answer to a question will probably create another step.

Tessa had helped me make the chart. She's very organized. Her mother says when Tessa was a year old, she took all the Pampers out of the box and laid them in neat piles on the bathroom floor. I think that's supposed to be a joke. But Tessa really is a great organizer.

Anyway, everything was all arranged with Buster ("He said, 'Oh, what a frolic!' " Tessa grumbled. "He's really weird!"), so we started on the questions. I had called Noah's Ark.

"Do you still have the three tarantulas?" I asked.

"No, we sold one this morning," Noah answered.

"Oh no! Not the black-and-orange one?" I yelled.

"No, we still have that one."

"Oh please, please don't sell it!"

"I'm sorry, without a deposit—"

"How much of a deposit?" I asked.

"Five dollars will do."

"Ask him how much the tarantula will cost. And what you should keep it in. And if crickets are really the best food . . ." Tessa went on.

"All right. All right." And that's when Noah told me I've got to have forty-four dollars and twenty-five cents, plus two dollars a month for crickets, which are the best food.

"Oh, Tessa, what am I going to do?" I asked again. "And what if he sells her before we get there? Couldn't we go this afternoon? I bet Buster—"

"Lizzie, you know I have a piano lesson in half an hour."

"Yeah. I'm sorry."

"Anyway, I don't think that that many people want pet tarantulas."

"Yes, but he already sold one—"

"Lizzie!"

"Okay, you're probably right."

"Now look." She showed me the list of questions. Two had answers. Next to "How much does t. cost?" Tessa had written: "Tarantula—$25. Supplies—$19.25 plus $2 per month."

"Per?" I asked.

"Each. You know, like percent."

"No."

She crossed out "per" and wrote "each."

And next to "What will L. feed it?" it said, "Crickets."

"That leaves 'How can L. get it home?' and 'Where will L. hide it?' "

"Stop calling me L.!"

She ignored me. "Well, you could carry it home in the tank. But then how do you sneak it into your room?"

"That's simple. I'll do it when Mom is at her exercise class or her pottery class. But Tessa, how am—"

"Good." She wrote down, "In tank during Ms. S.'s exercise or pottery class." "Now, what about hiding it?"

"Under my bed. Except on Fridays—that's when

Mom vacuums the house. I'll put it in my closet every Thursday night."

"Sure it will fit?"

"Yes. But Tessa—"

She wrote, "Under bed. Except Fridays." "This is great! We've answered all the questions."

"But Tessa!" I shouted. "Where am I going to get the money?"

"That's Step C," she answered. And on the big chart opposite "Step C" she wrote; "Get $40.68." She left the space under "Solution" blank.

"Well, what's the solution?" I almost shook her.

"That's what we have to work out. But I've got to go play piano."

My face must've looked upset, because Tessa said, "Don't worry. We'll think of something. Maybe your Aunt Tillie will leave you a legacy."

"I don't have an Aunt Tillie."

"That's just a joke."

I didn't feel like asking her what "legacy" meant.

4

Friday the Thirteenth. Actually, it's really Friday the Twelfth, but it might as well be the thirteenth because it's been the worst day of my life.

It all started in school today. Ms. Eggleston didn't say anything when she laid my report on my desk. She just clucked. But I know a bad cluck when I hear one.

"Oh, an E!" Julie Lindstrom exclaimed. "Thank you, Ms. Eggleston!"

"Don't thank me. You deserved it," Ms. Eggleston answered.

"What did you get, Lizzie?" Julie asked in a loud whisper and leaned over to see.

"It's none of your business," I growled, stuffing the paper into my knapsack.

"All right, don't tell me. But I bet you got another U, because I saw you at the library copying most of it out of the encyclopedia."

The class heard her and laughed.

After school, I told Tessa to pick me up at my house in half an hour. She looked at me funny, but said, "Okay." Then I hid behind a parked car and looked at my report. Bad news:

MEXICO
by Elizabeth Anne Silver

Mexico is the northernmost country of Latin America. It lies just south of the United States. The Rio Grande forms about two thirds of the boundary between Mexico and the United States. Among all the countries of the Western Hemisphere, only the United States and Brazil have more people than Mexico. Mexico City is the capital and largest city of Mexico. It is also the largest city in the Western Hemisphere.

There are lots of animals in

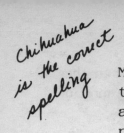

Chihuahua is the correct spelling

Mexico. (Chiwawa) dogs come from
there. And cows, bears, deer
and mountain lions, coyotes,
prairie dogs, alligators,
fish, birds, snakes and
especially iguanas and
spiders, (especially)
tarantulas.

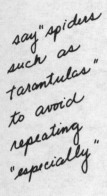

say "spiders
such as
tarantulas"
to avoid
repeating
"especially"

Tarantulas are really
interesting. They are hairy
and pretty. They can be very
big--ten inches including the
legs sometimes. They can live
up to twenty-five years, which
is very old. They can jump out
of a cage, so you have to have
a screen on top. They live in
tunnels and don't spin webs,
but they wrap the corpses of
their food and their poops in
silk. Tarantulas have many
enemies--birds, lizards,
snakes, rodents, tarantula
hawks and people like my
sister Rona. But tarantulas
don't hate people. Once on the
Johnny Carson show some guy
held up a tarantula and it

didn't bite him. The guy said
tarantulas make great pets,
and that's when I decided I
wanted one.
   Someday I'd like to go to
Mexico and see the iguanas and
tarantulas and the other
animals too. But not the
bullfighting because that's
disgusting.
The End

Lizzie,
   You have copied half of this
report out of the <u>World Book
Encyclopedia</u>, and the rest of
it is not about Mexico but
tarantulas. Although tarantulas
are indeed interesting animals,
they are not the proper subject
for this report. Ⓤ

21

I got real mad and threw my report in a garbage can. I knew if· my mom found out she'd have a fit. And today of all days I didn't want her to have one. So I made sure I had a big smile on my face when I walked in my door.

"Hi, Mom. I'm home. I'll skip the milk today because Tessa is coming over to . . ." But I didn't finish because my mom walked in with her thundercloud face on.

"Sit down," she said.

"Uh . . . Buster is—" I began.

"I said sit down, Elizabeth."

Uh-oh. Elizabeth. She only calls me that when she's really angry.

I sat.

"I will get right to the point. Ms. Eggleston just phoned me. She told me she had to give you an Unsatisfactory on your latest report for her and that it's the third U you've gotten this marking period, which is the final one. I didn't know you were doing so badly. I haven't seen a single one of those reports. Elizabeth, what have you done with them?"

"I . . . I . . ."

The doorbell rang.

"I'll get it!" I jumped up.

"Sit down!" Mom yelled. She was really angry. You see, she was a teacher for a while, and she takes school really seriously. "Just a minute!" she hollered in the direction of the door. "Well, are you going to answer me?"

"I threw them away," I said in a little voice.

"You threw them away? Haven't you heard of learning from your mistakes?"

That's when I started to cry.

"Oh, Lizzie." Mom sighed. "What am I going to do with you? Don't you like school?"

I didn't want to tell her the truth, that no, I hated it, because I knew that wasn't the answer she wanted to hear. I just cried harder.

The bell rang again.

"Mom . . . Tessa . . . Buster . . ."

"I'm sorry, Lizzie. You can't go with them. You're going to spend this afternoon studying for the grammar test Ms. Eggleston says you're having on Monday. She says you haven't been doing well on tests either—except in science."

"But Mom . . ."

She answered the door.

"Why, Ms. Silver, it's always such a pleasure to see you," Buster's voice boomed out. Buster always sounds like he's singing.

"Hi, Ms. Silver," Tessa said.

"Hello, Mr. Brown. Hello, Tessa."

"And where is my niece's charming friend—your

delightful daughter, Gloriana."

Gloriana is what Buster always calls me. He said that Queen Elizabeth I was named that in a lot of poetry and such. Tessa raises her eyebrows whenever he says it, but I think it's kind of pretty.

Buster swept into our living room and saw me. One look at my teary red face and he knew something was wrong. I stopped crying when I saw him. I had to—he looked so funny in a red-and-white-striped jacket, white pants and a straw hat. The stripes made him look even taller than he is—and he is very tall. When he took off his hat, I saw that his hair was all stuck flat down on his head. He looked like someone in an old-time barbershop quartet.

"Oh, Buster, who are you this time?" I asked.

"Buster Keaton, of course," he said. "If you keep smiling I'll take you and Tessa to one of his movies this evening."

"I'm afraid Lizzie can't go out with you and Tessa today, Mr. Brown. She has some studying to do."

Tessa, who had come quietly into the room, stared from Mom to me. "You can't go?" she blurted out.

I lowered my head.

"Oh, Lizzie!"

"Oh dear," said Buster.

"Mom, can I please talk to Tessa alone for five minutes?"

"All right. But just five minutes. Mr. Brown, would you like some juice?"

"I would be thankful for a draught of your nectar."

Mom blushed. "Apple or orange?" she asked.

"Oh, Eve's fruit, most certainly," Buster said.

"Yes, well, uh . . . come into the kitchen."

"Oh, Lizzie, how could you?" Tessa said furiously when we got to my room.

"I didn't plan it! Eggleston gave me a U and Mom found out."

"I told you to work on that report!"

"I did work on it. And stop sounding like my mother!"

"But now I have to spend the afternoon alone with Buster!"

"He's not so bad. He's funny. And it's nice that he lets us call him Buster instead of Uncle Buster. For an uncle he's kind of interesting. . . ."

"He's weird. Always dressing up like a different character. Just because he was nicknamed Buster because his last name is Brown. Everyone always stares at us. Mom says be happy he doesn't show up as Buster Crabbe."

"Who's that?"

"He was a famous swimmer."

I laughed.

But Tessa didn't. She was really mad.

"Tessa, don't be mad. I really want to go. I've got to get my tarantula."

Tessa hurrumphed.

"Listen, will you give Noah my deposit for me? Please? Pretty please? I'll do anything you want. Anything!"

"Tessa, time to leave," Mom called.

"Please, please, Tessa." I got down on my knees and bowed to the floor. "Please!"

"Stop that!" Tessa yelled.

"Please!"

"Oh, all right. I'm stuck going out with Buster anyway," she grumbled.

I jumped up. "Oh, Tessa, I love you. What do you want me to do in return?"

"I don't know. But I sure won't ask you to write *my* reports. I'll think of something."

"Okay. Here's the money. Remember, it's the black-and-orange one."

"I know."

"And tell me all about her and about Noah later."

"All right. All right. And you better *do* that studying. I don't want to go through this again—even for my best friend."

We walked out of my room.

"Thank you, Ms. Silver, for that divine potation. Ah, there you are, my dear." Buster reached for Tessa's hand. She scratched her nose with it. He turned to me. "Well, Gloriana. I am sorry you cannot step out with us. Perhaps next time . . ."

"Let's go, Buster," Tessa said.

"All right, my dear. Toodle-oo," he said to us.

"Toodle-oo." I waved.

"What a strange man," Mom said after she closed the door.

I grinned.

But soon I began to feel real bad again. Mom was mad at me. And that meant Dad would be mad too. And Rona was sure to be really obnoxious. Tessa was mad. Ms. Eggleston was mad. I couldn't see my tarantula-to-be. And, on top of it, I had to study boring grammar. But that wasn't the final straw. The final straw happened ten minutes later.

The phone rang. Mom had gone out to buy some food, so I picked it up.

"Hello, is this Lizzie?"

Oh no. "Hello, Julie," I said. "What do you want?"

"I just called to tell you I found something of yours."

"What?"

"Your report on Mexico. The one you got a U on. Someone must have put it in the trash can."

"Yeah. Someone must have," I said.

"Well, don't you want it?"

"Why don't you keep it? It might give you some

ideas for your next one," I snapped, and slammed down the phone.

Before the next two weeks are over, there are two things I'm going to do if they're the last things I ever do:

1) Get my tarantula.
2) Get Julie Lindstrom. And get her good.

5

I didn't get to talk to Tessa all weekend. I was still being punished and she didn't call. In fact, I didn't talk to her until lunch on Monday. She was still mad at me; she hadn't walked to school with me, and she wasn't going to sit next to me at lunch either except I went and stood behind her on line and whispered, " 'Better than,' not 'more better then.' "

She whirled around so fast her long curls slapped against her cheek. "What did you say? Oh, it's you."

"Yeah, it's me. I said, 'Better than,' not 'more better then.' "

"What *are* you talking about?"

"I studied grammar for two hours on Friday."

Her face got softer, but she said, "So?"

"Oh, come on, Tessa. Everybody else is mad at

me. Are you going to stay mad too?"

She looked at me for a solid minute and shook her head. "No. I'm not going to stay mad at you."

"Thanks, Tessa. You're my most best friend."

She sniffed. "I think you better study grammar for another two hours."

When we got our milk and pudding (we never buy the lunch—it's too disgusting) and sat down to eat, I said, carefully because I was excited, but I didn't want to get Tessa angry again, "So, how did your Friday go?"

Tessa made a face and took a sip of her milk. Then she said, "I don't understand how my sane mother could have such a crazy brother."

I sighed. It was going to be a while before Tessa decided to tell me about what I really wanted to know.

"Do you know, he kept taking off his hat like this"— she made a sweep with her arm—"and bowing and then putting the hat on his cane and twirling it around. People kept staring and asking if he was an actor or if he was selling something."

I put my hand to my mouth so I wouldn't laugh. I don't know why Buster gets her so upset. I would much rather spend a day with him than with a grammar book.

"He even bowed to the sea lions."

"The sea lions? What sea lions?"

"At the zoo."

"You went to the zoo?"

She nodded.

Then I started to get mad. "You went to the zoo and you're complaining . . ." But I stopped myself. "Well, it's nice that he took you to the zoo."

She just frowned. Then her face brightened up and she said, "There was a baby coati. It was so cute."

I bit my lip and swallowed hard. "Tessa," I said as calmly as I could, "the tarantula."

"What tarantula? There wasn't any tarantula at the zoo," she said, trying to look as though she didn't know what I was talking about.

"Tessa!"

Finally she said, "You ever hear of the installment plan?"

I sighed again. "Yeah," I said.

"Well, you just paid your first installment on a healthy, bona fide, black-and-orange Mexican tarantula." She grinned.

"Tessa!" I yelled. I reached over the table to hug her and spilled my milk.

"Girls." Mr. Dyson, the teacher on cafeteria duty, came waddling over. "You'd better clean up that mess."

I got up to get napkins, but before I left, I asked, "Tessa, is it beautiful?"

Her eyes were shining. "It sure is," she said.

We grinned at each other.

"And now, you have exactly two weeks from today to raise the rest of the money for it."

I stopped grinning.

"I've been thinking," Tessa said on the way home.

"About what?" I asked glumly. Even with all the studying, I don't think I did too well on the grammar test.

"About making money."

I perked up a little. "Yeah? Have you come up with any ideas?"

As usual, Tessa didn't answer directly. "Well," she said, "how does anyone make money?" She waited for me to answer.

"By going to work," I said.

"That's one way. Some people take in work."

"Huh?"

"You know, people who do sewing at home and stuff."

"But I'm not good at sewing."

She sighed. "Will you just listen?"

I was confused. "Okay," I said.

"Then there's performing—acting, dancing, singing."

"Isn't that like going to work?"

"Not really."

I didn't agree with her. "You play piano and you're always complaining about what a lot of work it is."

She thought about it for a minute and said, "Maybe you're right. . . . Anyway, there's also selling things."

"You mean like selling groceries or stuff? That's going to work, too."

"Ah, but what if you were to sell the stuff from where you live."

"From where I live? How could I sell groceries from where I live?"

"Not groceries, dummy," she said, exasperated.

"Don't call me dummy!"

She sighed again. "I'm sorry. But listen, what do people around here sell out of their houses all the time and make a lot of money from?"

I thought for a while and shrugged. "The only stuff I've ever seen anybody around here sell is junk."

"That's it."

"What's it?"

"We're going to have a junk sale, better known as a flea market."

"A flea market," I said. "A flea market!"

I thought about it. At first it sounded silly, but the more I thought, the more I liked the idea. Tessa and I have lots of old toys and books we could sell. And Mom and Dad and Tessa's parents probably have some junk they want to get rid of too. "I like it," I said. Then I started to giggle. "You know . . . ha-ha . . . what, Tessa? . . . Ha-ha . . . When I was little . . . ha-ha . . . I used to think . . . ha-ha . . .

a flea market was where they sold . . . ha-ha . . . fleas."

She smiled and said, "Well, this flea market is where they raise money for spiders."

"You said it," I said.

"Just cross your fingers it doesn't rain."

We smiled and linked pinkies on it.

6

It wasn't raining. In fact, it was a beautiful day, but Mom was giving me a little trouble.

"You know, Lizzie, I shouldn't be letting you do this. Not after the mark you got on that grammar test."

"But Mom, I passed it," I said, even though we'd been through this already.

"A sixty-five is just barely passing, Lizzie."

"Oh, let her do it, Mom," Rona said. "It's better than that stupid scientific junk she's always doing." She gave me a snooty look.

I gritted my teeth. I didn't want to yell and get Mom angry.

"Hey," Rona went on, "remember the time she didn't wash her feet for a week because she wanted to see how dirty they could get? You could smell them clear across . . ."

I couldn't keep quiet anymore. "I can smell you right now," I cut in. "Eau de Rat."

"Elizabeth, any more of that and you won't have any flea market today."

"But she started it, Mom."

She ignored me and said, "And as for you, Rona Silver, some things are better left forgotten."

The doorbell rang. "It's Tessa," I said, picking up the box I'd brought down from my room. It was full of old books, balls, jacks, games and a doll. The doll was in pretty good shape. My Aunt Minnie bought her for me, but I never liked her with her designer jeans and fluffy dresses. I offered her to Tessa, but she said she didn't need a doll that dressed even fancier than she did.

"Hey, you selling that Millie doll?" Rona asked.

"Yeah. You wanna buy it? Two bucks to everyone else, but for you, only three," I said.

Rona grunted, but Mom laughed. Then she said, "There's some things in the basement you can take. And I've got some old costume jewelry you might like. I'll bring them up and leave them in here."

"Thanks a lot, Mom," I said.

"And I'm sure Rona has some jun . . . er, things you can sell, too."

"I don't have anything," Rona grumbled.

"Why don't you take a quick look?" Mom said, and left.

"What about your old love letters from Charlie Peters? I'm sure he'd like to buy them back," I said.

Rona tried to swat me, but the bell rang again and I awkwardly threw open the door with the carton still in my arms.

Tessa had two big shopping bags full of stuff. "And there's more at home if we need it," she said.

"Great!"

"Hey," said Rona, getting an ice-cream pop from the fridge. "What's this sale for anyway?"

"What do you mean what's it for?"

"What's the money going to? What charity?"

"Charity?" I stuttered.

"Our favorite charity," Tessa said smoothly. "Us."

"You?"

"Sure. Kids need money too," Tessa said.

"For what?" Rona asked.

"Boy, you must really have a short memory," I said, following Tessa's lead. "For food, for books, for clothes, for . . . things."

Rona just shrugged and left the house. Maybe she thinks boys should pay for all that stuff and girls should just spend money on necessities like makeup and movie magazines.

Tessa and I went out and set up the folding table

and two chairs Mom told us we could use. I started just dumping things on the table, but Tessa said, "No, we have to make it look neat, attractive. This section for clothes. This for books. This for toys. This for household goods."

"Household goods?"

She pulled an ashtray shaped like an old boot and some plastic containers shaped like carrots and celery out of one bag.

"Ugh. Who'd want to buy that stuff?"

"You'll see," she said.

I shrugged and helped lay out things according to her system.

"Did you put the signs up?" she asked.

"Yeah. On the corners, on some lampposts, at the library and at the shopping center."

"Great. I put them up at the school, at Artie's candy store and some on lampposts too."

I took out a cigar box Dad had given me. "We should put some money in it so it looks good," I said.

Tessa dropped a quarter in. "That's my contribution to the P.T. fund."

"The P.T. fund?"

"The Pet Tarantula fund."

Just as we linked pinkies, our first customer came down the street.

"Hello, madam," Tessa said to this weird lady who

was wearing a heavy brown coat even though it was mid-May and seventy-five degrees out. "Can I help you?"

The woman didn't answer, just scratched her nose, picked up the boot ashtray. "I'll give you ten cents," she said with a voice like a frog.

"I'm sorry, madam, it's twenty-five cents," Tessa said.

I kicked her under the table.

The woman put down the ashtray and walked away.

"What did you do that for? That piece of junk isn't even worth a nickel."

"Watch."

The woman walked up the street. She stopped and studied the sidewalk. Then she turned and came back. "Fifteen cents," she said.

"Twenty," Tessa shot back.

"Deal," the woman said and handed us two dimes.

When she left, I hugged Tessa. "Our first sale!" Tessa looked very pleased with herself.

Pretty soon, another woman came along. I knew her—Darlene Lambersky's mother. She's pregnant, and she looked nice in her black-and-yellow maternity dress—just like a banded *Argiope* spider. She looked over some of Tessa's old clothes and bought two dresses at a dollar each. "Handmade," Tessa told her. After that a well-dressed man arrived and wanted to buy the Millie doll for his daughter.

"Five dollars with the clothes," Tessa said.

I winced.

"You must be kidding. I'll give you two dollars," he said.

"Four dollars," Tessa said.

The man shrugged, put the doll down and walked away. Only he never came back.

"Oh well. Sometimes it works and sometimes it doesn't" was all Tessa said.

After an hour, we had made six dollars and seventy cents and were very hot. I went inside to get us something to drink. Mom had left a big box on the floor and a smaller one on the counter. I looked into the big box—clothes, and *phew*, they smelled like basement. Better air them out first, I thought. I poured out some juice, and I noticed a daddy long legs climbing up the counter. Now, a daddy long legs isn't a spider even though lots of people think it is. You can tell the difference between it and a real spider because its body isn't divided into a cephalothorax and an abdomen; it's all one piece. I set down the glasses and reached over so the daddy long legs could walk on my hand and knocked over the small box. Diamonds, rubies, emeralds spilled all over the floor. Mom's costume jewelry. Funny how junky jewelry can look as pretty as the real stuff—at least I think it does, never having seen much of the real stuff. I scooped the jewelry back into the box, said good-bye to the daddy long legs and carried the box and the juice outside.

"Great!" Tessa said when she saw the jewelry. "This will really sell."

Another hour went by, but this time, sales were slow. Only three people came by and only one—Mr. Ricci—bought something: a book for ten cents.

"You want to break for lunch?" I asked.

"Okay," Tessa said.

But just then a blond woman we didn't know drove up in a car. She was very tall and very friendly. She looked over everything, but especially the jewelry, and she tried on a bracelet and a sparkly ring. She admired them on her hand for a long time. Then she made a funny little *hmmmm* noise and put them back into the box. "I'll give you ten dollars for this whole box," she said quickly.

"Ten dollars!" I gasped.

This time Tessa kicked me.

"Isn't that enough? I just love junk jewelry," the woman said.

"It's plenty," I said before Tessa could do her bargaining act.

The woman smiled, took out her wallet and handed me a ten. Then she picked up the box, jumped into her car and drove off.

"She was in a hurry," I said.

"So were you," Tessa said. "We could have made her pay fifteen dollars."

"It wasn't worth fifteen dollars."

"So what? Do you or don't you want your tarantula?"

"Shh." I clapped my hand over her mouth. "Look who's coming."

It was Julie Lindstrom, neat as ever in a blue sundress.

"Ugh," Tessa said through my fingers.

"Hi, Lizzie. Hi, Tessa. I thought I'd check out your *little* sale."

I wanted to punch her in her little head, but instead I said, "What would you like to buy, Julie? A scarf you can wrap extra tight around your throat—when it gets cold, that is."

"No, thank you. But here's a book you might want to keep," she said, holding up one of Tessa's old books. It was called *Mexico: Yesterday and Today.*

"Listen, Julie. Do you want to buy anything or not, because we're closing up for lunch," Tessa cut in.

"Not," Julie answered. Then she just stood there and watched while we packed things up, and only sauntered off when we went into the house.

"Oooh, she makes me so mad," I said.

"You shouldn't let her get to you. She's just a jerk."

We rummaged in the fridge and took out peanut

butter and things. We made sandwiches, ate and started to do the dishes. Mom came down with a couple more books and a silly felt hat, which Tessa immediately tried on. "You girls must be tired. Here, let me do the dishes."

We let her and went back outside and started to set up again. While we were doing that, Mom came out with a puzzled look on her face.

"Lizzie," she said, "have you by any chance seen my engagement ring? The diamond one?"

"No, Mom," I answered, putting a pair of Jordache jeans on the still-unsold Millie.

"I was sure I left it on the counter just now. . . ."

I was trying to sit Millie down, but her jeans were too stiff, when Mom's words hit me. "What did you say?" I asked slowly.

"I was sure I left it on the counter near the refrigerator just now. Or maybe it was when I did the breakfast dishes," she said.

Diamond ring. Counter. Daddy long legs. Diamonds, rubies, emeralds all over the floor. The blond woman admiring the . . . the . . . Oh no. It couldn't be. It just couldn't. "Did you look all over?" I asked, the way Mom always asks me.

"Well, maybe I should look again."

"Good idea," I said.

But when she went inside, I turned to Tessa. "Hey,

Tessa. How much does a diamond ring cost?"

"It depends. Two hundred, three hundred. Maybe more if it's a good one."

I gulped.

"What's wrong?"

I looked in the cigar box. Sixteen dollars and eighty cents. Good-bye, P.T., I thought. Then I asked, "Do you think a bank would give me a loan? 'Cause I have a feeling I'm about to be in debt for a long time—if I live that long."

Tessa looked confused.

"Well, they say you can get bargains at a flea market," I went on, "and boy, did someone ever get a bargain. One grade-A, bona fide diamond ring sold to the blond woman in a hurry for ten dollars."

"Oh no," Tessa said, biting her knuckles.

"Oh yes," I answered. "And oh no."

7

"Did you notice her license-plate number?" Tessa asked.

"No. I don't even know what type of car it was. Just that it was silver and big."

"It was a Buick," Tessa said.

"How'd you know that?"

"I always notice the make of a car."

I looked at her in surprise. I guess you learn something new about people every day—even about your best friend. Then I said, "That's a pretty common car, isn't it?"

"Unfortunately, yes. But I think I'd have noticed it around the neighborhood if she lived here."

"Well, she couldn't live too far away. We posted signs only around here."

"Yes, but she might have been visiting, or she might be somebody's friend who was told about our flea market on the phone, or she might have just been passing through on her way to Oshkosh or some place."

"Oshkosh is in Wisconsin. My mother's cousin June lives there," I said miserably.

"Well, you know what I mean."

"I know what you mean. You mean I'm sunk."

We were quiet for a while. Finally I said, "Did you know the dance called the tarantella was supposed to cure tarantism, a nervous disease people thought you got from the bite of a tarantula?"

"That was the European tarantula, right? Not the American one," Tessa said.

"I told you about the tarantella before, didn't I?" I said sadly.

"It doesn't matter," Tessa answered kindly.

"Hello, toots." The voice was familiar.

We looked up. It was Buster in a derby and a pin-striped suit. Toots! Buster changes his vocabulary along with his clothes. I looked at him with a question in my eyes.

"Buster Brown—my namesake and famous tap dancer," he answered, and did a little shuffle. The taps on his shiny shoes scraped on the concrete.

"Tarantism if I ever saw it," Tessa said. Then, to Buster, "Aren't you warm in that outfit?"

"Not really," he answered, wiping the perspiration from his forehead. "Well, maybe a little." He turned to me. "Gloriana, my cookie, what's the matter? You look like somebody forgot your birthday. That jive grammar test still bugging you?"

I shook my head.

Tessa shot me a "Don't-tell-him-anything" look (she hadn't even told him about P.T.—she asked him to wait outside the pet shop while she did an errand), but I said, "Listen, Tessa, we're not coming up with any ideas and Mom'll be out any minute and this can't get any worse." I paused while Buster waited. Then I told him what had happened.

He whistled. "Whee—oo. That is a problem, ain't it?" He got quiet and picked up an interesting blue bottle from the flea-market table.

"Hey, I didn't even see that before," I said. "Where'd it come from?"

"My dad donated it," Tessa said, looking very embarrassed.

"I'll give you five bucks for this," Buster said. "I liked it when I bought it for your old man's birthday. I still do."

I had to hide a smile.

"And five bucks should cover an ad in the local

newspaper," Buster continued.

"An ad?" Tessa asked, curious in spite of her embarrassment.

"Sure. 'Mysterious Blond Chick in Silver Buick Who Bought Box of Jewelry at Saturday Flea Market Please Contact . . .' etc. Something like that," Buster finished.

"Hey, that's a good idea," Tessa said, surprised.

"Course it is," Buster replied.

"But if she doesn't come from here, she won't read the local paper," I said.

"Well, then maybe you should put an ad in another paper, too—one with a larger circulation."

"How much would that cost?"

"Ten, maybe."

Good-bye, P.T., I thought once again.

Just then, Mom came out. "I've looked everywhere," she said. "You think it went down the drain or something?"

No, but I may soon go down the drain, I thought.

"Er . . . Ms. Silver, it appears there was a slight mishap," Buster said, falling out of character.

Tessa and I both kicked him.

"Yes," I said, "we broke . . . er . . . a . . . bottle."

"A bottle? A bottle of what?"

"A bottle like this one." I held up Buster's buy.

Mom furrowed her brow. "Oh. Well, I hope you cleaned it up."

"Yes. We did."

"Keep looking for your ring, Ms. Silver," Tessa said. "I'm sure it'll turn up."

"I hope so," Mom said, looking really worried. "Maybe it's caught in the trap under the sink."

"Yeah. Why don't you look there?" I said, too quickly.

Mom gave me a funny look and said, "Well, if you're finished with your flea market, why don't you start packing up? Your father will be back from the golf course soon and we're going out to eat."

"Okay," I said.

She went back inside, muttering something about checking the trap.

Buster looked from me to Tessa and back to me again. "There's an old saying," he said, "and it goes, 'You're bound to cry if you tell a lie.'"

"We didn't lie," Tessa said.

"Yeah. Well, the rest of the saying goes, 'Ain't nothin' so uncouth as not telling the truth.'"

"Look, Buster. We're going to use your idea and put ads in the papers. If that doesn't work, then maybe we'll spill the beans."

"Be careful the beans don't spill you," he said, and picking up his bottle, he did a quick flap-ball-change (two miserable years of Ms. Forrest's tap and ballet class taught me that) and waltz-clogged down the street.

"He's as graceful as a jumping spider," I said.

"How graceful is that?" Tessa asked.

"Pretty graceful—to another jumping spider. Come on. Let's put this stuff away and get to work on that ad."

8

I felt good this morning. I was having a great dream. There was a fire in a one-hundred-story building and people were yelling, "Help!" I was working like crazy in my laboratory on a special safety net that was made from spiderwebs. I finished just in time to bring the net over to the building. One after another, people jumped into the net and bounced up and down, yelling, "Wheeee!" When they were all saved, they all yelled, "Hooray," and insisted I be given the Nobel Prize for science. And I was. Then Mom woke me up for school and everything came flooding back and I felt just as rotten as I had before I fell asleep.

Tuesday. Only six days left. And I have no money, no tarantula and no sign of my mother's ring.

Yesterday Tessa and I spent three hours sitting by

the phone waiting to see if anyone would answer our ad. We had put the ad in two papers. It read:

Woman In Silver Buick Who Bought Jewelry Box At Saturday Flea Market Please Call 555–7902 After 3 P.M.

It cost us fifteen dollars, which left only a little under seven dollars in our P.T. fund. And it wasn't worth it. Nobody called at all.

Today I dragged myself through school. And at three o'clock there were Tessa and I once again, sitting by her phone.

"Maybe she's a slow reader. Or maybe she hasn't had a chance to call yet," Tessa said.

"Or maybe she's just going to keep the ring and never call us at all."

Tessa didn't answer.

"See, even you're losing hope," I said. I got up and took Verde the iguana out of his cage and let him skitter up my arm onto my shoulder. It tickled and I laughed, but I wasn't feeling cheerful. I kept seeing me getting walloped if Mom ever finds out about her ring. And when I wasn't thinking about that, I kept imagining poor lonely Ariadne in her cage, just waiting for me to take her home.

"Hey," I said suddenly. "I just thought of a name for P.T.—Ariadne."

"That's a pretty name. Weird, but pretty," Tessa said.

"It's from this Greek myth I read. Ariadne was a weaver. She could make the most beautiful cloth in the world. Well, the goddess Athena didn't like that too much because *she* was supposed to be the best weaver. So she disguised herself as an old woman and challenged Ariadne to a contest. Ariadne was stupid enough to say she would win and that she was better than anyone else, even Athena." I stopped talking because Verde was running across my neck and tickling me again.

"So what happened?" Tessa asked.

I put Verde back into his terrarium and said, "Well, Ariadne won all right. And then she lost. Athena got very angry and turned her into a spider and she got to spend the rest of her life weaving."

"Ugh. What a raw deal," Tessa said.

"Maybe. Maybe not. Being a spider doesn't seem like such a bad life," I said. Especially right now, I thought. "Anyway, tarantulas don't spin beautiful webs the way orb spiders do, but I think it's a good name anyway, don't you?"

"Yes. I like it."

"Except I'm never going to get her, am I?"

Tessa was silent for a minute. Then she said, "I've been thinking. Maybe we can get an extension if we pay another five dollars or something."

"Then what? Face it, Tessa. I'm never going to be able to afford Ariadne. I'm never going to get back Mom's ring. And I'm going to have to go without my allowance for the next twenty years to pay for it. And then I'm going to have to go to jail." I started to cry.

"Go to jail?" Tessa said. "Why would you have to go to jail?"

"Because I'm going to crack open Julie Lindstrom's fat head," I blubbered.

Tessa tried not to, but she giggled.

And with the tears still running down my face, I started to giggle too.

When we stopped, I said, "I've got to go home for dinner. And then I've got to study or Mom'll kill me. I probably have only a few days left to live anyway before Mom puts two and two together, but I'd like to enjoy the little time I have left." I gathered up my books and said, "Boy, I hope Mom and Dad have called it quits over the ring. I don't think I can face them if they're still looking for it."

On Saturday, after Tessa and I had written the ad in her room, I raced home and found Mom and Dad sitting at the kitchen table looking glum. They had practically torn the house apart looking for the ring. The pipe under the sink (what Mom calls the trap) was off and the refrigerator had been moved and someone had even taken the burners off the stove.

"The garbage," Dad suddenly said.

"The garbage," echoed Mom.

And they ran outside to ransack the garbage cans.

I felt terrible. I thought maybe I ought to tell them the truth after all, but somehow I just couldn't. Sunday was even worse. I kept seeing Mom sneaking peeks at the counter and Dad going through the bureau in the hall. It made me feel so bad I spent practically the whole day by myself at the playground, because Tessa and her parents had gone to visit her cousin. If the lady ever does call to return the ring, I'll have to find some way to sneak it into some spot where Mom will find it, but where she might also have overlooked it. Like the soap dish or something. It'll be hard. There aren't many places she's overlooked.

"I've got to go," I said again to Tessa. "If the lady calls, call me immediately."

Tessa nodded and said, "Don't feel so bad, Lizzie. I'm sure things will get better."

Suddenly the phone rang.

Tessa grinned and picked it up. I grinned back and gnawed my fingers.

"Hello," Tessa said in her most grown-up voice.

"Yes. Yes. I see. Tomorrow? Definitely. Three o'clock. Nine Webster Road. Got it. And thank you . . . er . . . Ms. Cleary."

I could hardly sit still while Tessa talked, and when she hung up I blurted out, "Well? Well? Tell me!"

"Ms. Cleary says she knows something about a box of jewelry her neighbor bought at a flea market on Saturday. This morning, she happened to be looking through yesterday's ads (she hadn't bought today's paper yet) for a good used vacuum cleaner and she saw our ad. We have to meet her tomorrow at three o'clock at Nine Webster Road. That's not far from school."

"Wow!" I said.

"Yes," Tessa said. "I think things are looking up."

The phone rang again.

"Gee, I hope it's not another ad answerer. That would mean the last one was a fake."

"Or this one is," Tessa said. She picked up the phone. "Hello. Oh, it's you. Lizzie? Yes, she's here." She put her hand over the mouthpiece and shrugged. "It's Buster. He wants to talk to you."

I took the phone.

"Gloriana, my dear. I do not wish to beat about the bush. Could you perhaps use a little moola?"

"Moola?"

"Scratch. Greenbacks. Money," he said.

At first, I just swallowed hard. Then I shouted,

"Money! Can I use money? You bet your straw hat I can!"

"Fine. It appeared to me the other day you were in need of the same. Now listen, my dear. Are you willing to work?"

"Work?"

"Yes. I have a friend who can use a bit of assistance. And I believe it's the kind of work you might enjoy."

"What kind of assistance?"

"Ah, if you will meet me tomorrow at Two Fifty-one Temson Place at three o'clock you will learn the answer to your inquiry."

"Oh . . . um . . . can we make it four o'clock? I have a . . . um . . . prior engagement."

"Certainly," said Buster.

"Great! That's Two Fifty-one Temson." I wrote it down on my hand. "Is it okay if I bring Tessa?"

Tessa was shaking her head.

"Most assuredly. If she cares to come."

"Great!" I said again. "And Buster, thanks a lot."

"Don't mention it," he said, and hung up.

"Tessa! A job! I'm getting a job! Boy, things really are looking up."

But this time, Tessa frowned. "Humph," she said. "If Buster's involved, I wouldn't be too sure of that. I wouldn't be too sure at all."

9

"Well, this is it. Nine Webster," Tessa said, as we arrived at the neat gray-and-white house with two big rosebushes in front of it. "Boy, I bet you're nervous."

Since I was biting my nails, Tessa's remark wasn't much of a guess. "Yeah," I said. "Are you?"

"Nah. It's very straightforward. We find out who the neighbor is and ask about the ring," she said, and rang the doorbell.

The woman who answered was plump and smiling. "Come in, come in, girls," she said. "Go straight into the kitchen. I baked some cookies. I hope you like chocolate chip."

"Yes, we do, Ms. Cleary," Tessa answered politely.

"Mrs.," she said sharply.

Tessa winced slightly and I jumped.

Mrs. Cleary smiled. "Sorry. I just don't go for that feminist stuff. Sit down. Sit down. Would you like some milk to go with your cookies?"

We both refused, but Mrs. Cleary poured out two large glasses anyway.

"Now, you tell me all about your problem, won't you?" she said.

"Well . . ." I began.

But Tessa interrupted me. "Why don't you tell us just what your neighbor said first, Mrs. Cleary?"

She gave Tessa a funny look, but then she smiled again and said, "You know, when I was a girl I liked to play detective too."

Tessa and I snuck each other a quick "Oh brother" look.

"My neighbor, Wanda Barton, who lives in the house behind me—the one with the disgraceful yard that you can see through this window—was bragging to her next-door neighbor about a bargain she got at a flea market on Saturday. A whole box of jewelry for ten dollars with some very interesting pieces in it. I was . . . er . . . tending my flowers when I overheard her conversation. I thought Wanda was bragging a little too much, so when I saw your ad yesterday morning, I called."

"What kind of car does she drive?" Tessa asked.

"A silver Buick," Ms. Cleary answered.

Tessa and I looked at each other and Tessa nodded.

"Did she mention anything about a ring?" I asked.

Mrs. Cleary thought a minute and said, "As a matter of fact, she did. She said the best deal in the whole lot was a ring. I distinctly recall her saying it's so pretty it could pass for the real thing."

I gulped and Tessa kicked me under the table.

"But you didn't see the jewelry, did you, Mrs. Cleary?" Tessa asked.

Mrs. Cleary seemed to pout. "No, I didn't. Listen, now it's your turn to tell me what this is all about."

I looked at Tessa. "Well," she said carefully, "we . . . er . . . accidentally sold a valuable ring at the flea market, and from what you've told us, we have reason to believe Ms. . . . er . . . Wanda bought it."

Mrs. Cleary looked excited. "I thought it was something like that. . . . She's like that. . . . She . . ."

Tessa cut her off. "Thank you, Mrs. Cleary, you've been very helpful. We'll just go and talk to Wanda." She stood up.

"No, don't do that," Mrs. Cleary said quickly.

"Why not?" I asked.

"Because she's not home."

"We'll come back later."

"She won't be around then either. She works late— until ten or eleven—for a magazine," Mrs. Cleary said with a *humph*. "Why don't you come back on Saturday morning. She's usually around at that time. And then you can have lunch with me."

"Saturday?" I shouted. "That's a long time from now."

"We'll do that," Tessa said. "And thank you again."

"You haven't touched your milk," Mrs. Cleary called as we headed for the door.

When we got outside, I frowned. "Whew, something strange is going on there."

"Yes. But she did seem to know what she was talking about. Maybe we should try Ms. Barton's today anyway."

I looked at my watch. "Oh, Tessa. I've got to hurry and get to Temson Place before four o'clock. You're sure you don't want to come along?"

"I'm sure. You can let me know what happens. Look, I think I'll ring Ms. Barton's bell anyway—just in case."

"Okay," I said.

"And Lizzie. Ariadne's really a very pretty name."

I grinned at her.

Two Fifty-one Temson Place was a big rickety house that had been painted pink a long time ago. Now the paint was peeling and the porch was falling apart. I walked up the steps carefully, avoiding a broken one. There was no bell, but instead a brass door knocker shaped like a lion. I bit my lip and wished Tessa didn't hate her uncle so much. Then I took a deep breath and knocked.

I waited awhile. No one answered. I knocked again.

"Coming! Coming!" sang out a deep voice.

The door opened and there stood a little man with slicked-back black hair and a black cape. "Come in, my dear, come in," he said. Then he smiled and I could see his two big fangs.

"Holy trap-door spider!" I yelled and backed away. "Buster! Buster!"

"I'm right here, Gloriana," Buster said, coming up the steps behind me. "Hey, Henry, what are you trying to scare a young lady for? I thought you had better things to do."

Henry's mouth opened wide and his fangs hit the floor. "I'm so sorry," he said, fumbling for them. "I forgot. I've been wearing this all day. Trying to get used to the costume, you know. I didn't mean to scare you, my dear."

"It's okay," I said, still breathing funny. "I wasn't scared. Just surprised."

"As well you should be," Buster said drily.

I looked at him and noticed he was wearing a regular shirt and jeans. He looked younger, and I realized he was kind of good-looking. In fact, he looked a lot like Tessa's grandfather, whom I met last month.

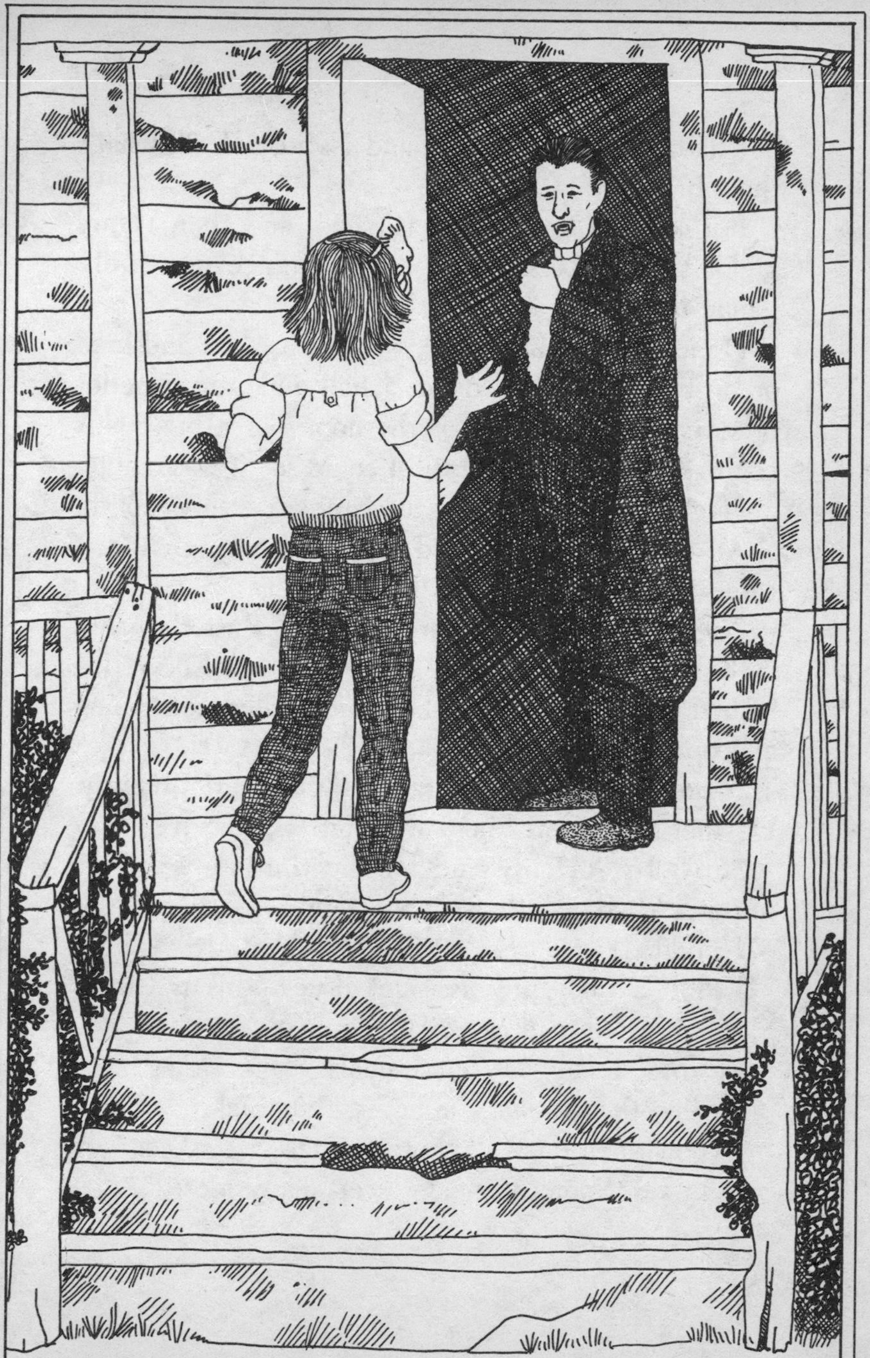

I had caught my breath, and I said, "Well, what's the job?"

Both Buster and Henry laughed, and then Henry said, "I like a person who doesn't mince her words. Come in and I'll show you."

He led us into his house, which was dark and kind of dusty. We walked down a hall and into a parlor of sorts. In the middle of the floor was a big, black coffin. The lid was open and I could see it was empty.

"Ugh!" I said, clapping my hands over my mouth.

All of a sudden, I heard a faint knocking. And it came from somewhere in the coffin.

"Oh, no!" I shrieked and grabbed Buster's hand.

"Oh dear," said Henry. "I've forgotten Lucy." He rushed to the coffin, pushed and pulled something and opened the lid.

A pretty blond woman sat up. "Good grief, Henry. Do that once more and I will quit! I swear it!"

"So sorry," Henry said for the third time in five minutes. "Lizzie—that is your name, right?"

I nodded.

"This is Lucy, my assistant. Lucy, this is Lizzie. She's going to take care of the animals."

"I am?" I said. "What animals?"

"Why, the rabbits, the doves, the chicks . . ."

"Wow! You have all those animals?" I asked.

"Oh yes. Some magicians keep many more."

66

"Magicians?"

"I see you're confused. Buster, you didn't tell the young lady who I am." He shook his finger.

"No, I thought she would enjoy a surprise."

Henry turned back to me and smiled. "Henry Markham, otherwise known as . . ." He swirled his cape. "Markham the Magnificent."

I stared at him. Buster gave me a tiny nudge and I applauded.

"You've never heard of me, have you?" Markham asked sadly.

"Well, not exactly," I said. "But I'm not really up on magicians."

"Will you help me out of this thing?" Lucy grumbled.

"Sorry, my dear," he said, and gave her his hand.

When she got out of the coffin, we all walked to the backyard. Markham had coops and cages all over the place. "This is Flopsy, Mopsy, Cottontail and Peter," he said, introducing me to the rabbits. "Lavinia, Josie and Fritzi." He pointed to the doves. "The chicks don't have names. And here we have Little Flower." He lifted out a small skunk. "Don't worry. He's tame and deskunked."

I petted Little Flower's head. He closed his eyes and yawned. "Do you have any tarantulas?" I asked.

"Nah. Too hard to manipulate. Although with this

new act . . . Nah. I do have a boa constrictor, though. Sparkle. She's inside. You'll meet her later."

"Wow! A boa! I love boas!" I said.

"Good. Now I'll tell you about the job. You see, I'm very busy, what with my new act and all. Count Markham the Magnificent, it will be called. I come out with this cape and these fangs. . . ." He stuck the fangs in his mouth. "And I say, 'Goot Evening. . . .'" The fangs slipped out again. "Oh dear," said Count Markham.

"I think you ought to can the fangs," said Lucy.

"Anyway," Markham said, "I need someone to feed the animals, clean the cages, et cetera. Does that sound like something you'd like to do?"

"Wow! You bet I would!" I said.

Buster smiled and Markham said, "Splendid. You may start tomorrow at, shall we say, three-thirty? Saturdays I'll need you earlier, say one o'clock."

I nodded.

"The pay is three dollars a day, Monday through Saturday—you get Sundays off—all expenses paid."

"All expenses?"

"A joke, my dear," Markham said.

I was figuring it out in my head. Three dollars times four days—five if I counted Monday—would give me fifteen dollars. But I needed almost eighteen more before I could get Ariadne on Monday. I frowned.

"Is something wrong?" Buster asked. "Don't you want the job? Won't your mother approve?"

"No," I said, then quickly, "I mean, yes. Yes, I'll love the job!"

This time, everyone smiled.

I did too. I figure things are looking up so much that maybe tomorrow it'll rain dollar bills. Or maybe Aunt Tillie will leave me that legacy after all.

10

Mom was inspecting the toaster.

"Your ring's not there, Mom," I wanted to say, but I didn't.

Mom was looking tired. "Only a few days more, Mom, and you'll have your ring back," I wanted to say, but instead, I just buttered my toast.

Mom put down the toaster and said, "Lizzie, I need you to run an errand for me after school. Ms. Schild-kraut was . . ."

"I can't," I interrupted quickly.

Mom gave me a funny look. "You can't? You don't even know what the errand is."

"She probably has plans to build the atom bomb in somebody's basement," Rona said.

"No, I don't, smarty-pants. It just so happens I've

got . . ." A job, I almost said, but I caught myself. "A lot of studying to do," I finished.

Mom was surprised.

"You're going to study?" Rona said. "I'll believe that when I see it."

"Well, you won't see it because I'll be studying at the library."

"Lizzie, that's wonderful to hear," Mom said. "But Ms. Schildkraut is right near the library, so before you go there, you can stop at her house and pick up the P.T.A. raffle tickets."

I frowned. I didn't want to make Mom angry— not after I had sold her ring and everything. But Ms. Schildkraut's house is blocks away from where Markham lives. In fact, they're in opposite directions. It would be bad to show up late for work on my first day. I might be able to make it to Ms. Schildkraut's first and then get to Markham's by three-thirty if I ran the whole way, but it'd be an awfully tight squeeze. "How about if I stop at her house after I finish?" I asked.

"No. She has to leave at three-thirty for a class."

Maybe I could ask Tessa to do it—no, she's done enough favors for me. I even owe her one. I frowned again, and asked, "Why can't Rona do it?"

Then Mom frowned. "I'm surprised at you, Lizzie. You've never complained about doing a simple errand for me before."

I knew I was getting Mom angry and that I should shut up, but I was getting angry too. "Why *can't* Rona do it? She never does anything."

"I have to go to the dentist, that's why. If you want to go for me, I'll pick up the g.d. raffle tickets."

"Watch your language, Rona," Mom said.

"I am watching it. If I weren't I would've said god . . ."

"That's enough. Elizabeth, you will pick up the tickets. Rona, you will go to the dentist. I will go shopping. Your father will remain at his office. . . ."

Rona cut in, "The president will remain in the White House, the bears will remain in the woods, the leaves will remain on the trees . . ."

"And the dogs will remain with their fleas," I finished.

Rona and I looked at each other and tried not to giggle, but we did anyway.

Mom sighed. "I give up. You two, finish your breakfast or you'll be late for school." She picked up the blender.

"Yes, ma'am." Rona saluted.

"All right, Mom." I sighed.

I was so excited about my job for Count Markham the Magnificent that I didn't even care when Ms. Eggleston announced that our final report of the term is "Your Favorite Poem and What It Means to You" and Julie Lindstrom leaned over and said in a loud voice, "What are you going to write about, Lizzie? 'Eensy, Weensy Spider'?" The class laughed—even Ms. Eggleston had to fix her face so she wouldn't giggle—but I just ignored them and thought about how I would be able to make friends with and study all of Markham's animals. I was thinking about experiments I could do with them—like do girl rabbits eat faster than boy rabbits and do skunks try to spray you even when they have no spray—when the bell rang for lunch.

"Want to come today and meet the animals?" I asked Tessa as I bit into my sandwich.

"No, not today. Let them get used to you first. I'll come along next week. . . . Listen, how are you going to work there on the weekend if you don't tell your mother?"

"I just will. I don't tell her everywhere I go."

"I hope you know what you're doing."

"Don't worry, I do." I changed the subject. "So Ms. Barton really wasn't home."

"No, she wasn't. And *Mrs.* Cleary was keeping an eye on me the whole time."

"What do you mean?"

"She actually followed me around the block."

"You're kidding."

"No. She pretended she was visiting someone next door to Ms. Barton, but I know she was watching me."

"But why? Why would she do that?"

"I don't know. Maybe she's just nosy."

"Yeah, probably."

"Anyway, I left a note for Ms. Barton to call and said if she couldn't, we'd visit her on Saturday at eleven o'clock."

"Oh, that was a good idea."

"I thought so myself," Tessa said, blowing on her nails and polishing them on her chest.

I blew her a raspberry.

When the last bell of the day rang, I picked up my books and sprinted out of my classroom and down the hall.

"Hey, Lizzie, where's the fire?" Mr. Jackson, the art teacher, called after me as I streaked past him.

And Marty Bernstein, the hall monitor, tried to stop me, but I made it out the door before he could blow his whistle.

I got to Ms. Schildkraut's house in five minutes and congratulated myself as I rang the bell.

But I stopped congratulating myself when no one answered.

"Oh rats," I said, sitting down on the stoop.

Five minutes passed. I was doing some figuring in

my head. It would take two minutes for Ms. Schild-kraut to park her car, a minute to open the door, two minutes to give me the tickets and ten minutes for me to run to Markham's house if I really pushed it. Fifteen minutes. I looked at my watch. Ten minutes past three. I could wait five minutes more. . . .

Finally Ms. Schildkraut pulled up in her car. "Sorry I'm late, Lizzie. I had to pick up the tickets at the printer's. Have you been waiting long? Would you like some . . ."

"Please, Ms. Schildkraut. I'm in sort of a hurry. Could you just give me the tickets?"

"Well, just a minute. I have to write down the numbers of the booklets on my sheet."

While Ms. Schildkraut carefully wrote down the numbers, I bit my nails, shifted from one foot to the other and peeled the cover off my arithmetic book.

"Here you are, Lizzie. Don't lose them," Ms. Schild-kraut said.

"Thank you, Ms. Schildkraut. I won't," I yelled, grabbed the tickets and raced off.

Puffing and panting, I got to Markham's house exactly on time.

"Oh good, you're right on time," Markham said, beaming at me. "I like an employee who's on time. In my line of work, timing is very important. Well, come in. My assistants are waiting for you."

Still too out of breath to say anything, I just nodded

and followed Markham into his backyard.

He told me what everybody eats and showed me where the food is kept, and watched as I filled the rabbits' and doves' dishes and changed Little Flower's Kitty Litter ("Skunks can be toilet trained easily," Markham said). "What about Sparkle the boa?" I asked after I watched Little Flower eat his hamburger meat.

"Ah. Sparkle only eats twice a week. Tuesdays and Saturdays. She had her mouse yesterday. I buy two mice every Saturday and keep them in this cage with food and water."

"Too bad," I said. "I wanted to see how fast she swallowed the mouse. Now I'll have to wait until Saturday."

Markham smiled. "You're really interested in how animals behave, aren't you?"

"Yes."

"That's good. Very good. Then you are very observant?"

It was a question, so I answered, "I guess so."

"Good." He reached toward my ear and pulled out an egg.

"Wow! How did you do that?"

"Observe carefully." He put the egg into his own ear and it disappeared. Then he opened his mouth, and out came the egg. "See?" he said.

"No, I didn't see! How *did* you do that?"

But he just smiled and said, "Magic, my dear, magic."

He cracked the egg and there, inside, was a key. He wiped it with a red silk handkerchief and handed it to me. "In case I'm not here sometimes, you can just let yourself in to feed the animals."

I smiled a big smile. Markham trusted me. He really did. I wanted to hug him. "Thanks," I said.

"You're very welcome. I can tell you and my assistants will get on just fine. . . . Now, would you like your wages daily or in one lump sum at the end of the week?"

I thought about it for a minute and then said, "In a lump sum at the end of the week. That way I won't spend it."

"Very practical," he said, and walked me to the door. Good day, Lizzie. See you tomorrow."

"Bye-bye," I said cheerfully.

I couldn't stop grinning all the way home. I grinned and skipped, grinned and skipped. He likes me. He trusts me, I thought. I'm going to work real hard and real good, and Ariadne, I'm going to take you home real soon.

It wasn't until I reached my door that I realized I'd left the raffle tickets right next to Sparkle's cage.

11

"Lizzie, is that you?"

I gulped and my voice came out in a squeak. "Yes, Mom." I walked into the kitchen.

She was peeling potatoes. "Did you have a good study?" she asked.

"Yes. Very good."

"Want some milk?"

"No. If it's okay, I think I'll go over to Tessa's until it's time to eat." I started to edge out the door.

"It's okay. But before you go, give me the raffle tickets."

I pretended I hadn't heard her and headed for the door.

"Lizzie!" She came after me just as I got the door

open. "Lizzie. The raffle tickets. Give them to me before you leave."

I had to think fast. "Oh no!" I said, slapping my cheek. "The tickets! I left them in . . . in the library."

"Oh, Lizzie." Mom sighed.

"I'll go back and get them," I said quickly.

"It'll be quicker if I just drive you over."

"No! Don't do that!"

Mom put her hands on her hips. "Why not?"

"Um . . . you've got things to do," I said. "I can take my bike."

Mom gave me the fisheye. "Elizabeth, you did pick up those tickets, didn't you?"

I looked straight into her eyes. "Of course I did. You can call up Ms. Schildkraut if you don't believe me."

Mom smiled a little. "Okay. I'm sorry. I believe you. But next time, put them in your pocket so you don't lose them."

"I will. For sure," I said.

"Whew," I breathed as I wheeled my bike out of the garage. After all this exercise, I ought to sleep like a log tonight, I thought. I got on my bike and rode off as fast as I could.

I could hear the shouting all the way out in the street, but I couldn't make out the words until I climbed the rickety steps.

"And another thing—you promised you'd remember my birthday this year and you forgot it again!" a woman's voice yelled. Then she started sobbing.

"I'm sorry, my dear. Really I am. Listen, this Saturday afternoon we'll do something nice, I promise. We'll have a picnic and go boating. You know how much you like picnics."

"You have a . . . matinee . . . on Saturday," the woman answered, still crying.

"I know. We'll go before my matinee. We'll meet at ten o'clock at the boathouse—"

"You'll forget . . . I know . . . you will."

"No, my dear Lucy. I won't. I promise I won't."

"If you do, I swear I'm going to quit. You've done this to me once too often."

"I know, my dear. And I'm terribly sorry." There was a pause, and Lucy said, "Oh, Henry, what am I going to do with you?"

And then nobody said anything.

I didn't want to disturb them, in case they were kissing or something, but I really needed those tickets and I couldn't stand there all day, so I knocked on the door.

Markham opened the door. He looked tired and confused. "Oh, hello, Lizzie. Weren't you here just before?"

"Yes, Markham. I'm so sorry. . . ." I stopped. I

was beginning to sound like him. I smiled and went on, "I left some raffle tickets next to Sparkle's cage."

"Oh. Well, why don't you run in and get them." He held open the door and I scooted in.

I caught a glimpse of Lucy in the living room. She was brushing her blond hair and sighing a lot. She didn't look at me, so I just walked to the back room. Sparkle was snoozing, and the tickets were right where I'd left them.

"Did you find them?" Markham asked, as I passed by the living room again. I noticed he was sitting next to Lucy with his arm around her. But he stood up when I came by.

"Yes. Thanks."

"Would you like me to buy a ticket?"

"No, thanks," I said quickly. You have to write down the person's name and address on the ticket stub, in case they win, and I knew I wouldn't be able to explain who Henry Markham is to my mother. "They're my mom's," I said. It was a dumb explanation, but he didn't question it.

"Well, see you tomorrow then."

As I walked out the door, I heard Lucy say, "That little girl is such an ugly duckling, isn't she?"

I didn't stick around for Markham's answer.

12

"You've been rushing out of school awfully fast these past few days, Lizzie," Julie Lindstrom said, sliding into her seat and carefully pulling her yellow dress over her knees. "Are you being punished or something?"

"No, I'm not being punished. And it's none of your business, anyway."

Julie's face got that sly look I can't stand. "Don't tell me you've gotten a boyfriend. Does he have buck teeth just like you?"

I was sticking my tongue out when Ms. Eggleston walked into the room.

"Watch out the flies don't land on your tongue, Lizzie," Ms. Eggleston said.

"Oh, she wouldn't mind that. After all, spiders eat flies," Julie said.

"There's this guy in *Dracula* who eats flies, but I forgot his name," Tommy Fredericks said.

"How do you know that?" Sarah Leibel asked him.

"I saw the movie."

"All right, class. This is a fascinating discussion, but it's time we got to work. There's a teachers' conference today, so you all get out at one instead of three. And we have plenty to cover in four hours, so open up your arithmetic books to page sixty-two. . . ."

I didn't want to, but I glanced at Julie. She was grinning at me. Just like a tiger shark. Which is maybe the only animal that I wouldn't want to meet face-to-face.

After school, Tessa and I went and sat on the kiddy swings in the playground even though we're too big for them. It was hot out and we were feeling goofy. And besides, I had this idea I wanted to talk to Tessa about and I figured we'd be left alone there.

"Markham and Lucy have any more fights yesterday?" Tessa asked.

"No. She wasn't around. She's what my mom would call a 'lulu.' "

"Lucy Lulu," Tessa said.

"Lulu Lucy," I replied.

We laughed.

"Hey, why don't you go there early today? Then we could go swimming afterward."

"That's a good idea—if Markham says it's okay. But I can't go swimming. I've got something else to do afterward."

"What?"

"Well, I've got this idea, see. To get the rest of the money for Ariadne."

"You do? Tell me!"

"Well, you know there's this P.T.A. raffle? The first prize is a TV set or something. Anyway, Mom gave me two books to sell to the librarians and teachers and anybody else who wants to buy them."

"Yes. So?"

"So the tickets are a dollar apiece. If I can sell eighteen tickets, I'll have enough to pay for Ariadne."

"But Lizzie, that money isn't yours."

"I know that. I thought maybe I could just borrow it until a week from this coming Monday—Mom doesn't need the money until then. Then I'll have earned eighteen dollars at Markham's and I can pay it back."

"Lizzie, don't you think you might get into trouble? As if you're not in enough of it already!"

"Awww, Tessa. I've just got to get Ariadne, and no more money has turned up."

"What about an extension? Now that you know you'll have the rest of the money in a week, Noah might give you an extension."

I was doubtful, but I said, "Well, it's worth a call."

"Okay. There's a pay phone around the corner. I've got a dime." Tessa climbed out of the swing and started to walk away.

"Hey, I'm stuck!" I shouted.

Tessa came back and tugged me out of the swing. While I was rubbing my sore rear end, she said in a high voice, "Why, Elizabeth, you're getting so big these days. I do believe you're becoming a woman."

I looked at her and snorted. "Why, Tessa Marie, I do believe you're becoming a 'lulu.' "

We laughed and headed toward the phone.

"You call," I told Tessa.

"Okay." She dialed and waited and said, "Hello. Noah's Ark? This is the girl who left the deposit on the tarantula. I was wondering if . . . What? Yes. Monday. Yes. I'll be there just as I promised. Okay. Thank you." She hung up. "Noah said, 'I'm glad you called. You *will* be here on Monday to pick up the tarantula, won't you, because there's someone here right now asking to buy it.' "

"Oh no." I sighed.

So did Tessa. "Well, I don't like it," she said, "but it looks like since Plan X—The Honest Approach— failed, we'll have to go ahead with Plan Z—The Dishonest Approach."

"I'm only *borrowing* the money, Tessa!"

"I know. But I still don't like it. Look, you call Markham and see if you can go there early. Then I'll help you sell the tickets."

"You will? Boy, you are the best, Tessa."

We linked pinkies and she said, "And that's two favors you owe me, Lizzie Silver."

I sighed and hoped I wouldn't owe her too many more before we were through.

Nobody answered when I knocked on Markham's door—Markham said he was probably going out when I phoned him—so I let myself in with the key.

I fed the animals and cleaned the cages, and then I went to watch Sparkle for a while. Markham told me I could pet her, and maybe next week I could take her out of the cage. She was wide awake, slithering up the glass, with her tongue flicking in and out. To-morrow she'd get her mouse, and then she'd probably go to sleep again for a few days.

" 'A narrow Fellow in the Grass Occasionally rides,' " a voice behind me said.

"Oooh!" I jumped, then whirled around.

It was Buster in a fancy blue jacket with silver buttons, white pants and a sort of captain's hat.

"Buster Mosbacher," he said.

"Who?"

"Buster Mosbacher, yacht racer."

"Oh." I shrugged.

"I am sorry I startled you. This house is so quiet."

"Yeah, it is. But I kind of like it. Markham forgot to tell me you'd be here."

"Yes. That sounds like him. I've been here all afternoon doing some research in his library. He has an excellent library, you know. Perhaps the largest collection of books on magic in the state."

"Wow! Where?"

"In the attic. You should ask him to show it to you."

"Did you get that line from one of his books?"

"Which line?"

"What you said when you startled me."

"Ahhh. Not from one of Markham's books. It is from a poem by Emily Dickinson."

"A poem? How does it go?"

"I can't remember the whole thing."

"Tell me the part you remember."

Buster smiled and recited:

> "*A narrow Fellow in the Grass*
> *Occasionally rides—*
> *You may have met Him—did you not*
> *His notice sudden is.*"

"What's it about?" I asked.

"Do you really want me to tell you?" Buster said. "Or would you like to think about it for a while and try to figure out the meaning for yourself?"

I thought a minute and said, "I guess I'll think about it for a while."

We watched Sparkle a bit, and I said, "Buster, there's something I want to ask you. How come you always dress up in these funny outfits? I mean, you're kind of good-looking. . . ." I stopped, embarrassed.

"You mean I'm not good-looking in these clothes?" he said with a grin.

"No, I didn't mean that. It's just . . . well, people are always looking at you like you're weird or something."

"That's true, Gloriana. And that's just what I want them to do. I like to confound people's expectations."

"What do you mean?"

"People expect other people to look, act, dress a certain way. They expect that so much that when they see anything out of the ordinary they think, 'How strange.' But at least they're thinking! They can't just sit back and relax and pretend it's—I'm—not there. They wake up a little. I like to wake people up. That's what I hope my writing does, too."

"Your writing? I didn't know you were a writer."

"Yes. I'm afraid not a very well-known one, though."

"Can I read something by you sometime?"

"Certainly, Gloriana. Anyone who thinks I'm good-looking deserves to read my work."

I laughed. And so did Buster. Then I looked at

my watch. "Oh, I've gotta go. I've got a lot of stuff to do. . . . Say, Buster, would you like to buy a raffle ticket for a worthy cause?" I wouldn't have trouble explaining Buster to my parents.

"What's the cause?"

"The P.T.A. They want to buy new curtains for the auditorium or something."

"Very worthy indeed," Buster said.

I couldn't tell if he was kidding.

"How much are they?" he asked.

"A dollar each."

"Fine. I'll take three."

"Three! Gee, that's great!" I gave him a booklet. "Write in your name, address and phone number." When I took the booklet back, I saw that he had written "Clovis Brown" in big letters with fancy squiggles. "Clovis?" I said. "I can see why you want to be called Buster."

He laughed and handed me the three bucks.

I handed him his part of the tickets and said, "I hope you win. I really do."

"Perhaps I will. I feel lucky today," he said, with a wink.

I winked back and went out to meet Tessa at school.

13

"We did it! We did it!"

Tessa and I were jumping around, hugging each other. In less than half an hour we had sold seventeen dollars worth of raffle tickets! It was so easy. We stationed ourselves at the two exits of our school and caught the teachers just as they came out of the conference. They told us how "sweet," "adorable," "conscientious," and "school spirited" we were to be selling raffle tickets for the P.T.A. We ran out of tickets before we ran out of teachers!

"Let's get some ice cream. We deserve it!" Tessa said.

"What'll it be, girls?" Jeremy Rabinowitz said as we stepped up to the cool white counter. "Cones?"

"I just got my allowance. Let's hit the big time," Tessa said.

"Sundaes?" I said, my mouth watering.

"Sundaes!"

"Triple scoop?"

"Triple scoop. My treat."

"Hot dog!" I said. Turning back to Jeremy, I ordered a chocolate-pistachio-strawberry sundae with all the trimmings and Tessa ordered the same.

"You sure that isn't too much for a little thing like you?" Jeremy said to Tessa. He didn't say anything to me. Nobody ever thinks I'm too little to do anything except most of the things I want to do.

"I'll manage it," Tessa said.

Jeremy shrugged and made the two sundaes.

We carried them carefully outside and sat on the curb to eat them.

"Yum-my!" Tessa said, gobbling hers down.

For a little person, she sure eats plenty. I think she eats more than me.

"Hey, Ms. Barton never called, did she?" I asked. I'd been so busy with my job and everything, I hadn't even thought about her.

"No, she didn't. We'll have to go there tomorrow."

I felt a little tingle of nervousness, but I shrugged it away. "Boy, I hope she still has the ring."

"Me too," said Tessa, spooning up the last of her

chocolate syrup. "You going to finish yours?" She eyed my sundae hungrily.

"Yes, I am—and haven't you had enough?"

"Me? Never," she said. "Hey, we better go. It's time for my piano lesson."

"Okay," I said, quickly finishing my sundae. "Let's go."

When I got home, I was feeling pretty good except for my stomach, which was kind of stuffed. Nobody else was around, so I decided that maybe a little studying wouldn't hurt me. I picked up my reader and opened it up, looking for a poem I could write about.

Wild and free, the wild birds sing.
Wild and free, let our freedom ring.

That one didn't do much for me. I turned a couple of pages.

Little Lamb, who made thee?
Dost thou know who made thee?

Dost thou care? I sighed and leafed quickly through the rest of the book.

There is no Frigate like a Book.

Huh? What did that mean? A frigate? Wasn't that some sort of ship? There is no ship like a book? I think I'd rather ride on a sailboat than an encyclopedia any day. I laughed at my own joke. I was just about to close the reader when I noticed that the frigate poem was written by Emily Dickinson. Wasn't that who wrote the poem Buster recited part of? How did that go again? Something about a narrow fellow riding in the grass? I like the sound of that, even though I don't know what it means. "A narrow Fellow in the Grass" something "rides."

I heard my door open and in came Mom. She had a big smile on her face.

"Lizzie," she said, giving me a hug, "you really can be so responsible when you want to be."

I smiled back, but I had a funny feeling inside that something was about to collapse.

"I ran into Mr. Jackson in the supermarket . . ."

Uh-oh.

". . . and he told me how you and Tessa sold all of the raffle tickets I gave you to the teachers as they came out of their conference. What a brilliant idea!"

Double uh-oh.

"And since you did such a great job with the teachers, I'll give you another two books to sell to the librarians you see every day."

I felt the chocolate-pistachio-strawberry sundae rumbling around in my stomach. "Uh . . . well . . . I don't really have time . . ."

But Mom ignored me and continued. "Oh, and give me the twenty dollars you made for safekeeping until Ms. Schildkraut collects all the money in two weeks."

"The twenty . . . dollars . . ." I stuttered.

"Yes. You sold twenty tickets, right?"

"Right. Yes. I mean . . . Oh, forget it." I pulled a crumpled bunch of dollar bills, as well as the ticket stubs, out of my pocket. "Here," I said, feeling the lump in my throat get bigger.

She peeled a dollar off the bunch. "For you. Don't worry—I'll replace it. I won't cheat the P.T.A. Treat yourself and Tessa to some ice cream."

"Excuse me," I said. I pushed past her and ran out of my room and into the bathroom. Then I threw up.

14

Mom almost didn't let me go out today. She thought I was sick on account of my puking up one chocolate-pistachio-strawberry sundae with whipped cream, chocolate syrup, sprinkles, chopped nuts and a maraschino cherry. But I convinced her I was feeling fine. Actually, I was feeling miserable—but in my head and not in my stomach.

"Well, I'm certainly glad you're not sick," Mom said when I appeared at the breakfast table.

"Never felt better," I said, while my head kept pounding, "Only two days left, only two days left."

"Hey, who the heck is Gloriana?" Rona said, coming in with the mail.

"Give me that." I snatched the thin, white envelope out of her hand.

"So she *does* have a boyfriend," Rona said snidely.

"Shut up," I growled.

"Who *is* it from, Lizzie?" Dad asked.

My whole family is *so* nosy. They never think you might not want to tell them your whole life story. As usual, I gave in. "It's from Buster," I answered.

"Tessa's uncle?" Rona said.

"Yes." I saw Mom and Dad look at each other and shrug. I excused myself so I could open the letter in peace. I don't get many letters, so I was kind of excited and curious. Carefully, I pried open the flap and pulled out two sheets of paper. The first sheet said:

Dear Gloriana,

I looked up all of the words to "A narrow Fellow in the Grass," so I am passing them on to you. Have you discovered what it means? Perhaps reading the entire poem will help you.

Although I can in no way consider myself in a class with Emily Dickinson, I thought, since I promised to let you read some of my writing, I would include one of my poems along with hers. I hope you enjoy them both.

See you soon. And Gloriana, keep shining.

Your friend,
Buster

I looked at the second sheet. On it, neatly typed, were two poems. The first was "A narrow Fellow in the Grass." I read the words silently and then out loud:

A narrow Fellow in the Grass
Occasionally rides—
You may have met Him—did you not
His notice sudden is—

The Grass divides as with a Comb—
A spotted shaft is seen—
And then it closes at your feet
And opens further on—

He likes a Boggy Acre
A Floor too cool for Corn—
Yet when a Boy, and Barefoot—
I more than once at Noon
Have passed, I thought, a Whip lash
Unbraiding in the Sun
When stooping to secure it
It wrinkled, and was gone—

Several of Nature's People
I know, and they know me—
I feel for them a transport
Of cordiality—

But never met this Fellow
Attended, or alone
Without a tighter breathing,
And Zero at the Bone—

I still didn't know what it meant, but somehow it made me feel kind of spooky. It sounded so chilly. "Zero at the Bone." I decided I'd read it again later. Then I looked at Buster's poem. It was very short and it rhymed and it didn't seem too hard to understand, except for this Russian name in it:

Palette

In summer I walk on diamond dust
Amidst Kandinsky blues.
In winter I flake off railing rust
And pour sand out of my shoes.

I read it out loud too. And when I did, I decided that maybe it wasn't so simple after all. I mean, it seemed to be about doing something in summer and something else in winter, but when I read it out loud, I suddenly got very sad and I didn't know why. I figured I better read that one again later too. I was just putting the envelope into my top drawer when Rona barged into my room.

"Don't you know how to knock?" I snapped.

Rona ignored my comment. "Tessa's here," she said.
"Tell her I'll be right out."

Rona nodded, but didn't budge. Finally, she asked, "So what does the letter say?"

"That's none of your business. I don't ask you about your letters, fathead."

"I'd tell you about them if you asked."

"Like fun you would," I said. "Now, if you'll excuse me, I have things to do!"

"Honestly, you're such a child." Rona sniffed and stomped out.

I thought a minute, then pulled out a long, straight hair from my head. I opened my drawer again and carefully laid the hair across the envelope. "Touch that, RonaBona, and you die," I whispered. I slowly closed the drawer and ran out to join Tessa so we could pay a visit to the famous Ms. Barton.

"What if she doesn't have the ring? What if she sold it? What if . . ."

"What if the moon turns blue? What if the sky falls down? Lizzie, you've got to stop being so nervous. Let's just get there first and hope everything turns out all right."

"Okay, Tessa." Then I yawned. I always yawn a lot when I'm nervous.

We walked up the slate path to the steps and up

the steps to the door. "You ring it," I said.

"You weren't this nervous last time we came here," Tessa said.

"I know. But that's because Mrs. Cleary called and everything. . . ."

Tessa shrugged and rang the bell.

While we waited, I yawned three times.

Finally, the door opened, and there she was. The mysterious blonde with the silver Buick.

"Well, hello," she said, opening her wide green eyes even wider. "You're the two girls who had the flea market, aren't you? This is a surprise."

"It is?" I blurted out.

"She means we left you a note," Tessa explained.

"You did? Where did you put it? I never got it."

Tessa and I looked at each other. "In between the screen door and the inside door," Tessa answered.

"That's strange. . . . Well, what can I do for you?" she asked, stepping out onto the porch. She didn't ask how we got her address.

"I . . . we . . . um . . ." I began.

"It's about the purchase you made at our flea market, Ms. Barton."

"Call me Wanda," she said. She didn't ask how we knew her name.

"Okay, Wanda. Well, about the jewelry you bought—"

100

"Oh, yes? That was certainly a wonderful bargain. Do you have any more you'd like to show me?"

"No!" I shouted.

Wanda gave me a funny look and Tessa glared at me. Then she said, "You see, there was a ring in the box—"

But before Tessa could finish, a police car screeched to a stop in front of Wanda's house. Two cops jumped out the front doors. And out of the back came Mrs. Cleary.

"Officer Foley, ma'am," a big cop said. "We have some information that you purchased a valuable ring for a low price even though you knew its worth. That constitutes an attempt to defraud two innocent children and may even be classified as theft."

Wanda looked from the officer to Mrs. Cleary, who had a big smirk on her face, to Tessa and finally to me. "I think I can guess where that note went," she said to me. Then she looked back at Mrs. Cleary. "So you had me staked out, did you?" Then she turned to Officer Foley. "I'll show you the ring I bought, officer," she said calmly, holding out her hand. There, on her index finger, was a silver ring with a big turquoise blue stone. I remembered seeing it in the box. It didn't look anything like my mother's engagement ring.

"Show them the other ring," Mrs. Cleary said.

"There was no other ring." Her voice was still calm.

"Are you sure?" Tessa asked.

"I'm sure," Wanda answered.

And somehow I knew she was telling the truth. I also knew she was really angry.

"We'd like to search your house, if you don't mind," the other cop—also big—said.

"But I do mind. Do you have a warrant?"

"Lady, we can easily get one," Officer Foley said.

Then I stood up. "No. No. You can't search her house. She didn't do anything. She bought that ring—and it was worth ten dollars, maybe a little more. But that's all. There was no other ring."

Officer Foley looked at Mrs. Cleary. "I thought you said these kids were willing to swear this lady swiped a diamond ring off them?"

"Listen, Wanda," Mrs. Cleary barked, "you can fool these kids, but you can't fool me. I know your type."

"And just what is my type, Ms. Cleary?"

"*Mrs.* Cleary to you, you . . . you . . . snob. You don't act like anybody else around here. You think you're better than me, just because you're a magazine editor and good-looking. And that magazine you work for—*Modern Woman.* Ha! You're so busy trying to unite all women, you can't even take five minutes to sit down and have a cup of coffee with me. You have no use for honest, hard-working housewives like me!"

Tessa and I didn't even look at each other. The hatred and loneliness in Mrs. Cleary's voice made us freeze.

For a minute, no one said a word. Then the other officer said, "Ma'am, I think there's been a mistake here. Sorry to have troubled you." He touched Officer Foley's arm. "Come on, Jim. Let's go."

Officer Foley didn't say a word. He just grasped Mrs. Cleary's arm and led her down the steps. It wasn't until he got to his car that he released her arm, and then we heard his voice boom out. "Thanks for making a fool out of me, Aunt Peggy." He and the other cop got into their car and drove away.

Mrs. Cleary stood, drooping, on the sidewalk. Then she straightened out her dress and, without looking in our direction, hurried down the street.

"Oh, Ms. Barton, we're so sorry," Tessa said. "The diamond ring . . . it's still missing. . . . We put an ad in the paper . . . Mrs. Cleary phoned. . . . She said . . . Oh, we're so sorry."

Wanda let out a dry little laugh. "Don't be. That woman has been pestering me since I moved here. I doubt she'll pester me anymore. So thanks a lot. You two have done me a favor." She walked back into her house, the door slamming behind her.

We stared at the door for a minute. "I don't think

she likes us," I said, shaking my head.

"That; Elizabeth Ann, is the understatement of the year."

I sighed and wondered how long it was going to take to save up for one diamond ring.

15

Tessa and I were staring forlornly at her chart spread out before us on the floor. The solution to Step C was still blank.

"Look, maybe that person who wanted to buy Ariadne won't show up again. Maybe nobody else will show up for the rest of the week. You could call up and say you've got the flu or the chicken pox or something and can't come in until you recover."

"Yeah, and have Noah say, 'Too bad. But those are the breaks'? No, thanks."

Tessa threw up her hands. "For goodness' sake, Lizzie. It's not as though there won't be other tarantulas."

"Just what do you mean by that?"

"If Noah sells the tarantula, we can find another one somewhere else."

"I don't want another tarantula. I want Ariadne!" My voice was rising.

"Lizzie! You haven't even seen her!" Tessa yelled.

"So what? I know just what she looks like! Some friend you are to let Noah sell Ariadne!" I hollered back.

"Girls, should I get out the boxing gloves now?" It was Ms. Lawrence, standing in the doorway to Tessa's room. "I've been knocking on this door, but you were so busy yelling you didn't hear me."

"Sorry, Mom," Tessa said.

"Normally I wouldn't interrupt such a private discussion, loud though it be, except that Buster is on the phone, and he says it is important that he talk to Lizzie."

I must've looked puzzled, because Ms. Lawrence said, "I don't know what it's about either—but you know Buster. He gets these fancies sometimes."

I followed Ms. Lawrence out into the hall and picked up the phone. She didn't hang around—which is one of the reasons I like her. "Hello," I said. I could barely hear Buster's reply because there was all this yelling in the background. "What did you say?" I shouted into the mouthpiece.

"Come . . . quickly . . . Markham's . . ." was all I made out.

"I'm not supposed to be there until one o'clock."

"Come . . . now," Buster shouted back.

I heard a click and I stood there looking at the dead receiver.

I ran back to Tessa's room. "Listen, something's up. I've got to get to Markham's on the double."

"What's the matter?"

"I don't know."

"I'll go with you."

"You will?"

"Lizzie, I'm still your friend."

I knew that was Tessa's way of making up. "And I'm still yours," I answered. That was my way.

We linked pinkies and raced out of the house.

You know about the thing they call *déja-vu*? When something happens and you think it's happened to you just that way before? Well, if Tessa hadn't been with me I would've said I was having *déja-vu*, because just as we got to Markham's house there was all this yelling once again, so loud you could hear it in the street.

"Wow, talk about boxing gloves!" Tessa exclaimed.

I nodded and said, "Watch out for the middle step. It's busted."

Tessa jumped over it and followed me to the door.

"You promised! You promised! Meet me at the park, he says. I show up with a loaded picnic basket and wait for two hours! Two hours! Does his highness ever show up? No! Well, that's it. The last straw. I said

I'd quit. And I'm quitting!"

"But Lucy. The matinee!"

Lucy said something really rude about what Markham could do with the matinee.

"I don't think I want to be here," Tessa said.

"It'll be okay. I think she does this all the time." I knocked real hard on the door.

I thought I heard a low voice, but I couldn't make out what it said. Then Lucy's voice screeched, "You stay out of this, Buster. You take his side all the time!"

There was silence, and Buster opened the door. He was wearing a pin-striped suit and a soft, slouchy felt hat—the kind Dad calls a fedora. From his vest dangled a gold chain. "Wow!" I exclaimed.

"Buster Brothers. Gangster," he said out of the side of his mouth.

"Terrific!" I said.

"Hey, glad you goils made it. Good ta see ya, Tessa, kiddo."

Tessa made a face.

"Come in," Buster said. "The joint is jumpin'."

"So we hoid . . . er . . . heard," I said. "Are you sure we're welcome?"

"You will be soon," he said, puzzling me.

Tessa and I walked in cautiously behind Buster. When we got to the parlor, we saw Markham, in his cape and slicked-down hair, on his knees. Lucy was standing before him in a fancy halter sundress with a small suitcase in her hand.

"Well, Henry Markham. This is good-bye. For keeps."

"Oh, Lucy. Please don't go. I beg of you. I am so sorry, my dear. And we do have a matinee."

"Like I said before, you know what you can do with the matinee." She turned to go.

"But Lucy. Think of all the children you'll be disappointing. And my dear, dear Lucy, think of all the good times we've had." He hobbled forward, still on his knees. It was embarrassing.

"You can do the same thing with the good times that you did with the matinee." With that she tossed her head and, brushing past us, stomped out the door.

Quietly, Buster ushered Tessa and me into the parlor. We sat down on the fat sofa and didn't say a word. Markham didn't say anything either. He just got off his knees and sat down on a fat chair, his head in his hands. Every once in a while he let out a moan. Finally, after what seemed like ages, he spoke. "She'll never come back."

"Sure she will," Buster said. "She'll be back by nightfall."

"Never. This time she's gone for good."

"You said that two months ago when she walked out."

"But she did that while we were on vacation. She's

never walked out on a show. I tell you, this time it is, as she said, 'for keeps.'"

"Now, now," Buster said, going over to Markham and patting his back.

"I'll never be able to work again. Not without Lucy. It's too late to get another assistant today. And if I miss the matinee, Virginia will fire me." He sunk his head into his hands again.

After about five minutes, with his head still in his hands, he said, "Um . . . just out of curiosity, what time is it?"

Buster took the gold watch attached to the gold chain out of his vest pocket. "It's twelve-thirty."

Markham sighed. "Too late," he said.

"I think you might be able to get another assistant in time for the matinee."

"Impossible," Markham said. "She'd have to get here, learn the routines and leave before two o'clock."

"What if she were already here?"

I held my breath. What was Buster doing?

Markham looked up. "What are you talking about?" Then he noticed Tessa and me for the first time. "Oh hello, Lizzie. Have you fed the animals already?"

"Not yet," I said.

Markham nodded and turned his head. "Now Buster, what was that nonsense you were saying about a new assistant coming here?"

"She *is* here. You just looked right at her."

Markham turned his head back slowly and stared at me with a blank look. Suddenly a gleam came into his eye. "Well . . . well . . . she *is* a good size," he said. Then he shook his head. "No, it'd never work. Too much to learn. Too little time."

"Try her, Markham. After all, you don't want to disappoint your audience. Try her."

"Yes, Markham. Try me!" I said.

"Well . . ." said Markham.

"Well?" said Buster.

"Well . . . I suppose it's worth a try. Would ten dollars be a sufficient wage for your services? I'm afraid that's all I can afford right now."

Tessa and I looked at each other.

"I'll take it," I said.

"I'll feed the animals," Tessa said.

"Oh dear, I forgot to buy a mouse for Sparkle," Markham said.

"I'll get one," said Buster.

After they left, Markham looked at me and said, "Welcome to the world of magic, little Elizabeth." And he pulled a flaming match out of my hair.

"Wow!" I said.

"Wow," he answered. "Now hurry. Let's get to work."

16

"I've made it as simple for you as I can," Markham said, while we—Buster, Tessa, Lavinia, Fritzi, Josie, Cottontail, Little Flower and I—were driving to the Magic Lantern. "No levitation, no elaborate disappearances. But I must leave in the sawing-the-lady-in-half and the dove-rabbit-girl illusions."

I nodded.

"What's he talking about?" Tessa whispered.

"I can't tell you. I swore I wouldn't explain how the tricks are done."

"That's the Magicians' Code of Honor," Buster said.

Markham smiled and said, "I'm also going to bring on most of my apparatus and items myself, so that you don't have to keep a lot of things straight. But I'll need you to take away Lavinia and Fritzi and Little

Flower, and to help me with the final illusion."

I nodded again.

"I'm sure you'll do well," Markham said.

I gulped.

The Magic Lantern is a small, dark, nightclub-type place that features magic and other assorted acts. It has a small stage at one end surrounded by tables and chairs. We set the animals down backstage, and Markham said, "Let me check the equipment and show you what I explained to you before." Suddenly, he paused and slapped his forehead. "Your clothes," he said.

"What about them?" I looked down at my jeans and T-shirt that said:

FAIR PLAY FOR SPIDERS

"A magician's assistant has to . . . has to . . ."

"He doesn't think your outfit has enough class," Tessa said.

"Oh," I answered.

Just then a pretty, red-haired woman came up to us. "Hi, Markham," she said. "How's tricks?" She laughed and touched his arm.

"Oh, hello, Virginia, my dear. Ah, Lizzie. I'd like you to meet Virginia Jamison, the owner of this club. She also helps me a bit with the act."

"Hello," I said.

"Hi." She smiled back. Then she looked at Markham. "You all set? Where's Lucy?"

"Uhhh . . . Lucy had an emergency . . . her mother . . . took sick. . . . She had to visit her. She'll be back . . . late tonight."

"That's too bad," Virginia said. But from the way she said it, I couldn't tell if she was happy or sad about it. "I thought she said her mother lives in Florida?"

"Yes. Well. Maybe she won't be back quite so soon after all. . . . Lizzie is going to be my . . . er . . . assistant. For today."

Virginia looked at me and said, "Hey, that's a great idea. Should go over real well with the kids."

I let out the breath I'd been holding.

"Well, honey, you better go change."

"Uh . . ." I said.

"Uh . . ." said Markham, "the thing is . . . well, this being an emergency . . . what I mean is—"

"She doesn't have a costume," Tessa said. "Have you got anything she can wear?"

"Are you another assistant?" Virginia asked.

"No. I'm Lizzie's friend."

"Oh. Well, I might have something. But we'd better hurry. It's ten to three. The show starts in fifteen minutes."

She took us to a little back room behind the kitchen. It was dusty and made me sneeze. "Oh, that Markham," Virginia said as she took down some boxes.

115

We rummaged around in them, pulling out pieces of lace and ruffles and other stuff.

"Hey, how about this?" Tessa said. She held up a tennis outfit.

"Now who could have left that here?" Virginia said.

"It's too big," I said, holding it against me.

"I have it," Virginia said, lifting down a box from the shelf. "The Leaping Lizards performed here. They really stank. But anyway, they left some costumes. I think they're in this box." She opened the lid. There were two of the brightest satin leotards I've ever seen in my life, screaming green and roaring red. They hurt my eyes.

"Perfect," Virginia said.

"Ugh," I said.

"She's right, Lizzie," said Tessa. "They're perfect for the act. Here, put on the green one. You'll look just like Verde."

I sighed and reached for it. Then I changed my mind and took the red one. "Better for vampires," I said.

Tessa grinned.

While I waited in what they call the wings, I alternately yawned, bit my nails and pulled at the bottom of my leotard, which was too tight and kept riding up into the crack in my backside. I could hear the mumbling of the crowd at the tables—well, it didn't exactly sound like a huge crowd; I couldn't tell how many people were there, but more than two was too many for me. At least Buster and Tessa wouldn't laugh at me if I messed up.

Suddenly it got quiet. The lights were going down and this eerie music was playing. Then the curtain opened and a spotlight hit the stage, lighting up the big, black coffin in the center. It was strange to see the whole thing from the wings. The audience yelped. Slowly the coffin lid opened, and with a jerk, Markham sat up. The audience screamed, but it was a happy scream.

"Goot evening. Count Markham greets you." He waved his hand and a flame shot out. "We are going to haff a bloody goot time," he said, climbing out of the coffin. His fangs slipped out and fell on the floor. He winced and kicked them under the coffin. I think the audience thought it was part of the act and applauded. Markham recovered his calm and went on with the show.

I watched while he did a trick with a candle, making it float in the air, then some tricks with red silk scarves that turned into balloons and rope tricks and coin tricks and tricks with big silver rings. It didn't have much to do with Dracula, but it was pretty neat anyway.

"And now," he announced, "I need an assistant from the audience."

A little boy, only about six or seven, got up onstage.

"And what is your name, young man?"

"Jonathan."

"Ah, are you by any chance Jonathan Harker?"

The boy looked blank. It took me a minute to remember that Jonathan Harker was the good guy in *Dracula*.

"Well, Jonathan, I'd like you to meet some of my friends." He pulled two rubber bats and three rubber spiders out of the boy's hair.

Jonathan giggled and said, "I want one."

Markham handed him a spider and sent him back to his seat.

"And now," Markham said, "for some more of my friends."

I swallowed hard. That was my cue. I got into place. Markham wheeled me and the box out. I heard the audience laugh when Lavinia appeared. Markham closed the box, spun it around and opened it again, and out came Cottontail. Louder applause. Close. Spin. Open. Da-da. I popped out, smiling, the way Markham told me to do.

The audience—which was about twenty people—cheered.

I curtseyed. Then Markham handed me Lavinia and Cottontail and I carried them offstage.

Whew! I breathed a sigh of relief. Only two more appearances to go.

Markham did some more tricks—this time with

cards and a pretty one with colored sand. Then he said he was going to do a variation of the rabbit out of the hat trick. He showed an empty top hat to the audience, and put it on the table. He reached in and pulled out, first, a big bottle of perfume, next a bunch of roses and finally Little Flower.

"P.U.," said the audience, even though Little Flower doesn't smell.

I came on and carried Little Flower off.

A few more tricks—changing water into fire and stuff—and then it was time for the big one.

"Ladies and gentlemen, boys and girls. For my final trick of the day—sawing the la . . . er . . . girl in half."

Applause. My stomach lurched. I wanted to run to the bathroom, but I stepped out onstage.

Markham helped me into the coffin and, leaving my head sticking out of one end, he closed the lid. I can't tell you exactly what I had to do, but let me tell you, it wasn't too comfortable being squished up like that. And it wasn't too comfortable for Virginia either, who, as Markham had said before, helps out with this part of his act.

Markham pulled out this big saw and started cutting. Then, he pulled the halves of the coffin apart and tickled the feet sticking out of the bottom half. I laughed like I was supposed to. The audience laughed too.

Finally he put the halves back together and waved his cape over them. When he opened the lid, I stood up and curtseyed again and the audience applauded a lot.

When the curtain closed, Markham hugged me. "You were splendid, my dear. So good, in fact, that I am going to teach you levitation. For tonight's show. And that'll be another ten dollars for you."

"Oh wow!" I said. "Twenty dollars! Ariadne! I can get Ariadne!"

Markham gave me a puzzled look, but didn't ask me anything. Then Buster and Tessa came backstage and Virginia joined us and they all hugged me, too. We all talked and laughed about the fangs and went into Virginia's dressing room and had Cokes. Virginia was teasing Markham plenty, the way a person does when she likes someone a lot. Markham finally got the message.

"Virginia, my dear, how would you like to go out for dinner tonight?" he asked.

Virginia's face lit up. "I'd love to, Markham," she said. "Lizzie, would you care to join us?" she asked politely.

"No, I think I'll have dinner at home and come back in time for the show." Only then did I realize that Markham expected me to perform from eight to ten o'clock and that my parents expected me to be in bed at nine.

17

"You could pretend you're sleeping over at my house and just sneak in at ten-thirty," Tessa said.

"Look, if I have to sneak into anyone's house I'd rather sneak into my own."

"If only Buster wasn't taking me and my parents to some dumb poetry reading tonight, we could get him to take us to the magic show—"

"That's it!" I said.

"What's it?"

"Buster will have an extra guest at the poetry reading. Me!"

"But Lizzie, your parents might call up my parents to confirm it."

"Not if your parents called them first," I said.

"What are you talking about?"

"Well, you know how you're always imitating your mother's voice . . ."

"No."

"No?"

"No. We'll both get into a lot of trouble. It's not worth the risk."

I looked glumly at Tessa and didn't say anything. Then I turned my head and sat staring miserably off into space.

"Oh, for goodness' sake, stop looking like that. I'll do it!"

"You will?"

"I just said I would."

"Oh, Tessa, you're so—"

"Three favors," she cut in.

It worked like a charm. My mother thought Tessa was Ms. Lawrence and gave permission for Buster to take me with the Lawrences to the reading and for me to stay up past my bedtime, but I was to be home at ten-thirty sharp. Then Mom told "Ms. Lawrence" to send me home for dinner.

"How will you get there?" Tessa asked me.

"Bus."

"Bus? Are you kidding?"

"No, it's not hard. I noticed that the J bus, which

runs right up the street, stops in front of the Magic Lantern."

"You're going to take the bus alone at night?"

"Only one way. Markham can give me a ride home."

"You're crazy."

"No. Just desperate," I said.

At dinner, Mom said that it was very nice of Buster to be so nice to me.

"He's a nice man," I answered.

"I thought Tessa didn't like him," Rona said.

"Well, she's getting to like him more and more," I said, wishing it were true.

"I'm sorry I don't have time to take you more places," Dad said. "But these sales conferences . . ."

I looked at him. He looked sad and tired and I realized he really hasn't been around much these days. When I was little, I used to talk with Dad a lot. He and I would go places alone and stuff. Not fancy places—just the playground or the movies or something—while Mom and Rona were at dancing school or having tennis lessons or whatever. I was always lousy at those things and Mom and Dad learned that pretty fast when Ms. Forrest, the dance teacher, told them maybe I should try flamenco, the kind of dance where you stamp your feet a lot, instead of ballet. Anyway, after we moved out of the city and Dad had to travel to work, we didn't get to do stuff together very much anymore. It made me sad for a while, but I'm kind of used to it now. I guess maybe Dad isn't.

"It's okay, Dad," I said.

He smiled at me.

I felt bad that I was lying to him—and to Mom—but I knew they'd never let me perform in Markham's act to make money to get Ariadne to be happy. They don't understand the scientific mind.

Rona was out at the movies and Mom and Dad barely looked up from the television when I said, "Bye-bye."

"Have a good time, sweetie," Dad said.

"Have fun, Lizzie," said Mom.

"I will," I answered, crossing my fingers behind my back.

There was only one other person at the bus stop, and fortunately it wasn't someone I knew—or who knew me. It was a bent old man with a cane. I wondered who he was, since I'd never seen him in the neighborhood, but I didn't feel like starting up a conversation.

The bus arrived pretty soon and I tripped on a step as I got on. Darn, I thought, I don't want anyone to notice or remember me, just in case. . . . Then I laughed at myself as I made my way to the back of the bus. In case of what? Who'd tell my parents anyway? And then I noticed Mr. Jackson, the art teacher, sitting in the last seat. And he had his arm around Ms. Martinez, the music teacher. And they noticed me, too.

"Oh, Lizzie, fancy meeting you here," Mr. Jackson said.

"Hi, Mr. Jackson. Hi, Ms. Martinez," I said.

Ms. Martinez blushed.

"Isn't this a bit late for you to travel alone on the bus?" Mr. Jackson asked.

"Well, actually . . . it . . . is," I stammered.

"I see," he said. "Well, perhaps we can make a deal. If you don't tell anyone you saw us, we won't tell anyone we saw you."

"It's a deal," I said.

Mr. Jackson and I grinned and shook on it. And Ms. Martinez blushed once again.

Virginia's eyes were sparkling. "I'm so glad to see you, Lizzie," she said.

I think she meant she was glad *not* to see Lucy. "Did you have a good dinner?" I asked.

"The best," she answered, and went off to see the electrician or somebody.

Markham was really happy to see me too. "It's going to be a fine show tonight. I can feel it!" he said.

"I hope so," I said.

"Are your parents coming to see you? They must

be proud to have a magician's assistant in the family."

"Well . . . actually . . . they're sick tonight."

"Sick? Both of them?"

"Yes, and my sister too. The flu."

Markham backed away. "I hope you don't get it and give it to me."

"Oh, I had it already," I said.

"You did? You haven't seemed ill to me this week."

"I had it a few weeks ago," I answered quickly.

Markham looked at me as though what I said didn't quite make sense. Then he shook his head briskly and said, "Let's go over the levitation routine once again, shall we?"

"Okay," I said.

The levitation routine was a little crazy. Markham would dramatically say, "Enter, Trilby" and then wave his hands. I asked who Trilby was, and he said some woman who got hypnotized a lot by some creep named Svengali. Anyway, when he said, "Enter, Trilby," I was supposed to come out with my eyes closed and my arms stretched out in front of me like I was sleep-walking. Markham taught me how to keep my lids lowered just enough so the audience would think my eyes were shut, but so that I could see the marks on the floor that told me where to go and not bang into anything. Markham would wave his hands again and I'd get real stiff. He'd lower my arms and he and Virginia, who came out to help, would hoist me onto this board perched on the backs of two chairs. More hand waving and Markham would remove the chairs. The board would appear to be suspended in the air, and Markham would make it rise. And the audience would applaude a lot.

I got into my red-satin leotard and waited in the wings. Tonight the levitation was going to be my first appearance—instead of the box illusion.

The lights were down, the spotlight hit and Markham did his coffin bit and the scarf tricks, coin tricks and ring tricks. The audience sounded larger tonight. And very enthusiastic. By the time Markham made a very sleepy Sparkle appear out of his cape (she enjoyed her mouse a lot, Tessa said) they were really excited. Virginia went out to get Sparkle. Markham didn't want me to get her because he said my appearance was to be a surprise.

More scarf tricks, and then it was time. I got into position, closing my eyes and holding my arms stiffly in front of me. Dramatic music from a scratchy tape.

"Enter, Trilby," Markham called. And out I came.

I got onstage without any goofs and let Markham lower my arms and get me onto the board. Away went the chairs. Up in the air I went. Markham walked underneath to show it was no trick even though it was, and the audience broke into loud applause. After that he lowered me and put the chairs in place, and he and Virginia helped me off the board. The audience applauded again. "Trilby, awake," Markham said, waving his hands again.

I opened my eyes, curtseyed and smiled broadly. I was feeling great. I had a new career ahead of me. I'd be able to buy a new ring for Mom sooner than I had thought. Then I noticed Lucy sitting right below. Good-bye, career, I thought, and curtseyed again.

The audience applauded furiously. Especially a girl at a table near Lucy. She was clapping and grinning like a tiger shark. She was Julie Lindstrom.

18

I don't know how I managed to get through the rest
of the show, but somehow I did. After I made my
final bow and the curtain fell, I rushed backstage and
into Virginia's room to change. When I came out,
Lucy and Markham were in the middle of making
up and Julie was waiting for me with her parents.

"Uh, hi . . . Mr. and Ms. . . . Lindstrom," I
stammered.

"Hello, Lizzie. You were just marvelous. Your parents must be very proud of you," Ms. Lindstrom said.

Mr. Lindstrom nodded in agreement.

And Julie kept smiling and didn't say a word.

"By the way, where are your parents? I didn't notice
them in the audience," Ms. Lindstrom said.

"They . . . uh . . . couldn't make it tonight. . . . The . . . flu."

"Really? Your mother seemed fine in exercise class yesterday."

"Well . . . it came on real sudden."

"Oh. Well, I hope she'll feel better soon. And your father, too. Well, let's go, Julie. We're getting up early tomorrow to visit Grandma."

"I'll be right with you, Mom and Dad. I just want to talk to Lizzie alone for a minute." She reached out and grabbed my hand.

Mr. and Ms. Lindstrom smiled the kind of smile that means "How cute. Julie wants to be alone with her little friend." "We'll meet you by the door," Mr. Lindstrom said.

Julie smiled back. So did I, even though Julie was squeezing my hand so hard I thought she'd break it.

As soon as her parents left, I said, "Let go of my hand, you creep, or I'll bust you in the chops with my other one."

Julie stopped smiling and dropped my hand.

I flexed my fingers. They hurt.

"The flu! Boy, you are a rotten liar!" she said.

I didn't answer her.

"I bet your parents don't even know you're here."

I still didn't say anything.

"Your parents don't know what you're up to at all.

But I do. I called your house on Thursday at four o'clock and your mother told me you were at the library. She said you spend every day at the library, studying. But I know you don't because *I* spend every day at the library. You were here, weren't you? Rehearsing or something."

"Ha! That's where you're wrong, Julie Lindstrom. I wasn't here at all," I said with what I hoped was a convincing sneer.

For a moment, it looked as though it was convincing enough. Julie didn't look so sure of herself. I was just about to lie and tell her I'd already left the library by four o'clock, but suddenly Lucy's voice rose loud and clear.

"Oh, Henry, I missed you. It's a good thing you got that little girl who feeds the animals to be your assistant. She was awfully good, even though she's so gawky—"

"Oh, Lucy, my dear, I too am glad you've come back . . ." we heard Markham say, and then his voice trailed off.

Julie turned back to me with a ferocious grin on her face. I winced and gulped. Julie saw and grinned harder. "So that's it. And you didn't tell your parents because you were afraid they wouldn't let you do it."

If there's one thing Julie Lindstrom isn't it's dumb.

"Listen, please don't tell my parents. They . . .

they . . ." I began, then I got disgusted with myself and lowered my eyes.

"Don't worry. I won't tell them. If . . ."

I picked my head up. "If what?"

"I don't know yet. I have to think about it. I'll let you know tomorrow."

"Julie . . ." Mr. Lindstrom's voice called out.

"Coming, Dad," she called back. Then she looked at me and said, "Tomorrow." She grinned once more and, with a toss of her horribly neat braids, ran off to join her parents.

"Oh, Lucy," I heard. "Oh, Lucy. Your eyes are so blue . . ." I sighed and turned toward the steps leading offstage.

"You need a lift somewhere, Lizzie?"

I looked up. It was Virginia. She looked as though she'd been crying.

"I don't think Markham will be leaving for a while," she said unhappily. "I don't know what it is that man has, but . . ." She broke off.

"He's got talent," I said.

Virginia laughed. "That he has, but I'm not sure that is what's so appealing about him." She laughed again and blew her nose.

I thought about how glad I am I don't like boys yet. I'm in enough trouble as it is without boys. "You going anywhere near Hillford Avenue?" I asked.

"Sure," she said. "It's not too far out of my way."

"Thanks," I said.

"Don't mention it. We troupers have to stick together. After all, there's no business like show business." She smiled a sad little smile.

I smiled back.

"You were a very good assistant," Virginia said.

"Thanks again," I replied, wishing I'd never met Markham, let alone been his assistant.

"You may have a future on the stage."

"I may not have a future at all," I muttered.

"What?" Virginia asked.

"Nothing."

"Well, let me just get my purse and we can go, okay?"

"Okay." Suddenly, because she looked so miserable, I wanted to say something nice. "Virginia, I really like your hair," I said.

"It's dyed. But thanks just the same."

"Don't mention it," I said.

Then she linked her arm with mine and we left together.

19

Sunday, and I was very nervous, waiting to find out what Julie was going to do. I hung around near the phone. It rang twice for me, but both times it was Tessa. She wanted to find out if I'd gotten home all right, which I had (I made Virginia drop me off at the top of the block, so Mom and Dad wouldn't notice her car in case they looked), and if everything else had gone all right, which it hadn't. I lied about the second part. That is, I didn't really lie; I just didn't tell her about Julie Lindstrom. I don't know why I didn't want to tell her. But I didn't.

"Hey, you want to go swimming today?" Tessa asked.

"No, I've got work to do. A report for Ms. Eggleston."

"You're going to spend a gorgeous Sunday working on a report?" Tessa asked, surprised.

"Yeah. Something wrong with that? You're always telling me how I should do my schoolwork."

"All right, all right. Don't be so touchy. I think that's great that you're working on your report."

"Yeah." I sighed.

"Lizzie, is something the matter?" Tessa asked cautiously.

"No. Everything's fine. Look, I've gotta go. I'll call you later."

"Listen, I called Buster."

"You did?"

Then Tessa got touchy. "Yes, I did. Someone had to arrange the trip to Noah's. You do still want to go, don't you?"

"Of course I want to go. Mom's got her pottery class tomorrow. Rona's got a dance class, so we can sneak in Ariadne easily."

"Good. Then I'll go with you to Markham's. Buster will meet us there."

"Great. See you then."

After I hung up, this big wave of happiness washed over me. I was going to get my tarantula after all. It was all arranged. Tomorrow Markham was going to pay me and then off we'd go—Buster, Tessa and me—to Noah's. I jumped up and started doing a tarantella, or at least what I thought was a tarantella. Then, when

I was out of breath, I sat down and read "A narrow Fellow in the Grass" again. "What *is* this about?" I said out loud.

And then the phone rang.

"Lizzie, it's for you," my dad called.

Slowly, I walked to the phone and picked it up. Slowly, I cleared my throat and said, "Hello."

"Hi, Lizzie. Are you alone?" the voice answered.

"No, Julie, I'm not."

"Okay, then just listen. I've figured out what reward I want for keeping your little secret."

"Reward?"

"Sure. You don't expect me to keep such a good secret for nothing, do you?"

If you were my friend, you would, I thought. But you're not. "Why do you hate me, Julie Lindstrom?" I asked.

"Hate you? I don't hate you. Whatever gave you that idea?"

Lots of things gave me that idea, but I didn't answer. I just sighed. "All right, what do you want me to do?"

"I want you to give up your job. And give it to me."

"What?"

"You should be in the library studying every day. You need to study. I don't. I'm getting all E's anyway. Besides, I need the money."

"You need the money! Your parents are rich! You can get anything you want! What the heck do you need money for?" I blurted out.

"What do *you* need the money for, Elizabeth Anne Silver?"

I was so angry, I felt tears welling up in my eyes, but I fought them back and said, "What'll you do if I say 'no'?"

"I'll tell your mother what you've been doing."

"Then I'll lose the job anyway—and so will you, because I'll tell Markham you're a narrow fellow in the grass!"

"A what?"

"A snake! A rattlesnake!" I hollered. "Except rattlesnakes are nicer than you. They only bite when attacked. You're not fit to take care of rabbits and doves and sweet snakes like Sparkle. Go on, tell my parents, rattlesnake! I don't care!" I slammed down the phone and spun around right into Dad's arms.

"What was that all about?" he asked.

"Nothing," I said. "It was about nothing."

"Lizzie, you know you've been acting a little strange lately. Is something the matter?"

"No. Nothing's the matter. I'm fine." I wriggled out of his arms.

"Lizzie, listen. I think you need a break from studying. How about if we take a walk together?"

"Later, Dad. Okay? I'd like to be alone for a while."

"All right," he said, frowning.

I walked straight out of the house over to Tessa's. Only no one was home. So I just kept walking to calm myself down. It wasn't until I got all the way to the post office that I realized I had figured out the meaning of Emily Dickinson's poem when I called Julie a snake.

"Hey, Elizabeth Anne," I said to myself, "maybe you're not so dumb after all." And I decided to go back home and do the report for Ms. Eggleston. Maybe I could do something right for a change.

By the time I got back, I knew just what I was going to write. I was even smiling when I opened the door to my house, and I kept smiling until Mom greeted me with her thundercloud face and said, "Julie Lindstrom just called. I think you and I better have a serious talk, Elizabeth. A very serious talk."

20

Darn that floorboard. The squeak was loud enough to wake Mom, who is a light sleeper. Sure enough, a light went on. I froze against the wall. It took me a minute to realize it came from Rona's room. Her door opened and she sort of stumbled out and into the bathroom. As soon as she closed the door, I tiptoed downstairs as fast and as quietly as I could. I slipped into the kitchen and got some apples and cookies and a package of Swiss cheese out of the refrigerator and stuffed them in my knapsack. When I opened the front door, it let out a creak. I waited to make sure no one had heard it. Then I closed it carefully and ran down the street.

It was very dark out—no moon, and the streetlights were dim. Things seemed to be moving in the shadows.

Cats. Or maybe muggers. What if I got mugged? I shivered. Well, at least then Mom and Dad and even RonaBona would feel sorry for me instead of hating me like they do.

Mom and I had had our "serious" talk. It was mostly Mom yelling at me and saying I lied, I cheated, I betrayed her trust, etc., etc. She said I was to come straight home from school from now on. She would call Markham and tell him I couldn't work for him anymore. She didn't even say anything about the fact that Julie Lindstrom was a rattlesnake and a spy and a blackmailer. Dad came in in the middle of it. Mom stopped and sort of started to tell what had happened and then went back to yelling at me again.

"Nora, you're not letting her get a word in," he said to Mom. "Look, Lizzie, is it true you have a job?"

I nodded.

Then Dad said, "Why didn't you tell us?"

"I didn't think you'd let me keep it," I answered, crying. "And I need it."

"You're darn right we wouldn't have. Not until you bring those grades up!"

"Nora, hush," Dad said. "Lizzie, honey, why do you need a job so badly?"

"I can't tell you," I blubbered.

"What do you mean you can't tell us?" Mom yelled.

Then Rona came in. "What's going on here? It sounds like a soap opera."

"Be quiet, Rona," Dad said sharply. "Look, Lizzie, I'm afraid your mother is right. You will have to be punished for this. I don't hold with ratting on people and I don't like children like Julie Lindstrom. She must have it in for you for some reason. And I know you must be furious at her. But the fact is you did do wrong, Lizzie. Believe me, we only want the best for you."

I wiped my eyes and felt my face grow hard. They always tell you it's for your benefit when you're being punished.

"Now, you go to your room. Your mother and I need to talk."

I went without another word.

After a few minutes, Rona came in. "Did you really appear in a magic show last night?"

I nodded.

"Well, kid, I've got to hand it to you. You sure have guts, but boy, did you ever blow it this time. What *do* you need the money for anyway?"

"Oh shut up, you . . . you . . . Nosy Nellie."

"Nosy Nellie! I'm only trying to help. Maybe somebody would have lent you the money if you'd asked nicely. Maybe I would have."

I looked at her. "You? You're always asking Mom for money so you can buy more lipstick and nail polish and blusher and eye shadow and whatever other garbage you buy."

She drew herself up very straight. "Well, Miss Priss, I know some people in this house all the lipstick in the world wouldn't improve."

"And I know some people in this house who read other people's mail."

Rona's nostrils flared and she said coldly, "I don't know what you're talking about."

"I just bet you don't," I said. I wasn't about to tell how I'd discovered the hair missing and the letter and poem put back out of order in Buster's envelope in my drawer.

She humphed and left. And I sat down and cried for a while. Then I decided what I was going to do. I dragged my knapsack out of the closet and packed some clothes, some paper and pencils, Buster's letter and all my savings. Then I hid the whole thing under the bed. Throughout dinner, no one said anything to me and I didn't say anything to them. When Tessa called, she was told I was not allowed to talk to her. Fortunately, no one seemed to have guessed that it was Tessa who had pretended to be Ms. Lawrence. I was glad about that. After dinner, I excused myself and went to my room. And then I waited.

I shivered again, even though it wasn't cold. I passed Tessa's house. It was as dark as the other houses on our street. My stomach growled; I hadn't been able to eat much supper. What was that noise? I whirled around. Nothing. Nothing at all. I sighed and kept walking. Past the post office and the supermarket. And I didn't see anyone the whole time, except for two cars. By the time I reached the school, I was really starved. I sat down on a swing in the playground and pulled out an apple.

"Hey, little lady, want to dance?" A long, thin shape rose from under the monkey bars. I yelled, dropped the apple and ran, nearly tripping over a bottle that probably belonged to the shape.

I kept running until I came to Markham's block. Then I stopped. Where was I going? What was I going to do? I hadn't thought out that part too well. I just wanted to run away from my house, my parents, my sister, but I had no place to go. Panting, I walked slowly to Markham's house, holding my side because I had a stitch in it. There was a light on in the parlor. I sat down on the porch steps for a minute and thought. Maybe I could talk to Markham. Maybe he could talk to my parents, tell them what a great assistant I was. It was worth a try. I knocked hard on the door and, right away, I was sorry I did. I didn't want to see Markham. I didn't want to see anybody. I ran down the steps and hid behind a bush. I waited a long time, but nobody opened the door. Then I realized that Markham's car wasn't in the street. Strange,

I thought, and put my hand in my pocket. In it was the key to Markham's house. Maybe something's wrong, I thought, and without thinking much more, I unlocked the door.

First I looked into the parlor. In the light, I could see Lucy's suitcase on the floor. Everything else was the same as the last time I saw it. I decided to check on the animals, and walked down the hall. When I got to the back room, I found the light switch and flicked it on. Sparkle was sound asleep. Next to her cage was a cage with a mouse in it, and next to that was an envelope that said: TO LIZZIE. I opened it and out came three ten-dollar bills and one five and a note that read:

Dear Lizzie:

Lucy and I have decided to take a little vacation. We will be back on Tuesday in time for the evening performance. Here is Sparkle's Tuesday mouse. Feed the other animals as usual. Here's your salary. You were a marvelous assistant. I'm very proud of you. And so is Lucy. See you soon.

Yours,
Henry Markham

Tuesday. Markham wouldn't be back until Tuesday. My brain started working. I could stay here and nobody would know. Then I said to myself, Be scientific, Lizzie. Mom and Dad know about Markham. When they find you've run away, this will be the second place they check—after Tessa's. You can't stay here. But nobody's home, my self answered. Nobody will answer the door. Yes, but suppose they call the police and get a warrant to search the house. Or suppose they get in some other way. You can't stay here. But you might as well rest awhile. I sat down and took out another apple from my knapsack. And as I bit into it, a bolt of lightning zapped through my head. Oh yes, you can stay here, Lizzie. You can stay in the attic. The library attic. They'll never look in the attic. All you have to do is find the way to get up there.

☞

21

There was no ladder or steps to the attic in the hallway of the second floor. So I decided the way to the attic had to be through one of the rooms. I opened the first door I came to. It was a bathroom. And it smelled a lot like a hair tonic my dad used to use when he was afraid he was going bald. The tonic didn't work. I closed the door and tried the next one. A closet full of weird clothes. No good.

I tried door after door, but none of them led to the attic. I was getting frustrated, so I decided to relax for a while by looking through the weird clothes in the hall closet. There were fancy suits, capes, gowns, coats with tails, clown outfits—all sorts of stuff. I guess Markham's act has gone through a number of changes. Or maybe he wasn't always a magician. I took down a blue spangled ball gown and held it against me. It felt nice. I put it back and then lifted out a purple-and-yellow clown costume. It had big pompoms and a polka-dotted ruff. One of the pompoms caught on a hanger and ripped off. It fell down on the floor of the closet. Oh no, I thought, and got down on my hands and knees and began to scrabble around for the pompom. I thought it had rolled into one of the weird shoes (to match the weird outfits) lying there, so I started shaking them out. Nothing. I crawled farther into the closet. There was a light bulb shining in there, but it wasn't bright and I couldn't see very well. I felt around on the floor. Something feathery tickled my face. I sneezed and banged my head against a round, hard shape. I reached out with my hand and grabbed it. It was a doorknob.

The door swung outward into a little landing leading to a steep flight of steps. I sneezed again, wiped my nose with the back of my hand, found a light switch and climbed up into the attic. Buster was right. Markham sure had one heck of a library. There were books everywhere, lining the shelves, neatly stacked against the walls. There were also magazines and colorful posters of magicians with names like Herrmann the Great and Blackstone. Some of the posters even showed illusions and said things like: "See the Vanishing Lady" or "Thrill to the Midnight Mysteries of the Yogi."

In one corner of the room was a trunk. In another was a small desk and a chair. And in the center was a cot. The funny thing was everything was so neat and clean. There wasn't any dust!

I glanced over the shelves. There were so many books I didn't know which to look at first. Then I saw one with a red cover that looked interesting. It was called *Baffling Illusions*. I took it down and opened it up and began to read:

During the Renaissance, the Decapitation Illusion was one of the most famous—and popular. A magician dressed as Harlequin beheaded an assistant in a clown costume at least twelve times a week, to the delight and amazement of the audience. The magician produces a long sword as the clown stretches out full-length on a block. Then, covering his assistant's head with a cloth, the magician proceeds to slice it off. While the onlookers gasp, the magician pulls off the cloth to reveal the headless body and the severed head. But this is not the end of the trick. The magician shows off the head, then wraps it back in the cloth and sets it next to the body. After a little song or two, Harlequin removes the cloth and tells the audience that this mischievous, wicked clown has been said to have nine lives like a cat, but that, finally, he is dead. While he talks, the clown's head begins to wink and wrinkle its nose and make other facial expressions until the audience is reduced to fits of laughter. When he notices the head's antics, the magician, feigning shock, flings the cloth over it once again and places it in its original position on the shoulders of the body. Then, suddenly, the figure rises, head and all, and, amid tumultuous applause, the clown, resurrected, dances before the crowd.

Wow, I thought, I wonder if Markham ever tried that trick! How was it done? I flipped through the book for the solution, but there wasn't any. Finally I got mad and almost threw the book across the room until I remembered that it wasn't mine. So I put it neatly back on the shelf where it belonged. Then I noticed a book next to it called *Baffling Illusions Explained*. I grabbed it and opened it quickly. Well, there were explanations all right, but they were for different illusions. Still, the book looked interesting, so I settled down to read it. But I felt myself getting sleepy. Oh well, I'll have plenty of time tomorrow, I thought, as I stretched out on the cot. Then I realized I had left the light on. It was kind of bright and I thought about getting up and shutting it off, but somehow I didn't want to sleep alone in an attic full of magic books in someone else's house in the dark.

I woke up because my stomach was growling real loud. Pancakes, I thought as I opened my eyes. "Hey Mom, can we have pan . . ." I started to say. Then I stopped. I didn't know where I was. All these books and this light burning . . . I thought I was dreaming or something until I remembered. The attic. Markham's house. How did I get here? Oh yeah, I ran away from home. And I felt as though someone had punched me in the gut. I, Elizabeth Anne Silver, had run away from home on Monday, May 29, the day I was supposed to get my P.T., Ariadne. I felt the tears form thick and hot in my eyes. No, Lizzie, you're not going to cry. You're not, I told myself. I took some deep breaths and forced the tears to stay where they were.

All of a sudden I heard a noise. It sounded like it was coming from the floor. Oh no, they've found me, I thought. It's all over! But then I heard a squeak, and a little gray mouse crawled out from a crack in the floorboards. It saw me, squeaked again and scurried off behind a bookcase. I giggled. And I felt a little better, but I figured I'd better go downstairs and clear away any evidence before someone did come to look for me.

I climbed down to the second floor and switched

off all the lights I'd left on in all the rooms. It was kind of gray out and I wasn't sure of the time. Six o'clock, maybe? So I was surprised when I went down to the kitchen and found out it was already after eight o'clock. I better hurry, I thought, they'll already have discovered that I'm gone. I went downstairs to the kitchen and made breakfast out of some cornflakes and milk and a mushy banana I found in the refrigerator. I was still hungry, but there wasn't much else to eat. I wanted to save my cheese for lunch. Then I checked on the animals, who were fine. I was thinking about lifting the mesh cover of Sparkle's cage so I could stroke her scales, when the phone rang. I jumped. I mean, I should have expected the phone to ring, but I hadn't. I stood there not moving and breathing as quietly as I could, as if the phone could see and hear me. *Ring ring.* "Shut up," I nearly yelled. I felt like I was going to reach out and grab the phone even though I had a feeling I knew who it was. So I put my hands over my ears and started to recite "A narrow Fellow in the Grass," which I had memorized—almost. Finally, the phone stopped ringing. *Whew!* I breathed a sigh of relief. But I knew it wouldn't be long before Mom or Dad or both of them showed up at the door. So I grabbed my knapsack and headed back up into the attic.

I tried to occupy myself by reading more of Markham's magic books. At first I had trouble concentrating, but then I started getting involved in what I was reading. The *Baffling Illusions Explained* book told me how to turn a goblet (which I think is some sort of a glass) of ink into an aquarium, how to produce a cake from an empty cake box and how to make a watch or a ring or a coin disappear. I especially liked the last trick. All you need is a box with a double bottom or a cylinder type thing with a false bottom. See, it looks like this:

False Bottom

You show this empty-looking cylinder to the audience—turn it upside down and all to show it's empty. But partway down is a phony bottom that opens with a spring. The lower half of the cylinder has soft stuff inside so the coin or ring or watch won't rattle. You could put the coin inside, press the spring and, presto, it's gone. Or you could show the empty cylinder, turn it upside down, press the spring and, presto, it's here! Anyway, I was reading about that trick when I heard a noise. It was faint but unmistakable. It was someone knocking on the front door.

I looked around for somewhere to hide, but then I realized I was already hiding. That's what I was doing in this attic in the first place! So I just sat there, feeling weird.

The knocking stopped. I wished there were a big window so I could look out and see if they had really left. But the little triangular one only looked out on the treetops. So I just sat some more and listened to my stomach growl some more.

The knocking started up again. I can't just sit here, I thought, so I decided to explore the trunk in the corner. It was a big trunk and kind of old, with a rusty lock and hinges. I tried to open it, but I couldn't. I sighed and was going to give up on it when I saw, hanging from a rusty nail, a little key. I took it and fitted it into the lock. The trunk lid opened with a groan. Inside was a white cloth covering something lumpy-looking. Carefully—in case it was fragile—I pulled aside the cloth, and there, staring up at me, was a giant spider. I yelled, "Wow!" and the lid slammed with a bang. Something else slammed too— but from farther away. It was the front door. Oh, no, I moaned.

"Lizzie, are you here?" a voice floated upstairs. "Lizzie!"

And there I was in the attic with a giant spider and with my parents downstairs below. It was what you might call a bad predicament.

22

My parents were slowly, methodically opening every door, looking in every room of Markham's house and calling "Lizzie, Lizzie!" even though they knew if I had wanted them to find me I wouldn't have run away in the first place. I couldn't figure out how they got in until I remembered that I'd forgotten to bolt the door last night—or rather, this morning. Man, that meant anyone could have come in—including that weirdo in the playground. I shuddered. The weirdo probably wasn't even as bad as my parents. They were right below me now, fumbling in the closet with the strange clothes. Please, please, I prayed, don't let them find the door.

They didn't. I heard the closet door slam and my parents move off to another door.

I sighed, opened the trunk and looked again at the stuffed spider. Funny, I like spiders a lot, but I have to admit that this one was kind of creepy. Maybe anything that's fifty times its normal size is creepy. I lifted out the spider carefully. It was a good job. I mean, it looked very convincing. Just like an *Achaearanea tepidariorum,* a house spider. But I couldn't for the life of me figure out what it was doing there or what it was for. I'll have to ask Markham when he comes back, I thought. Markham. What am I saying? He'll never let me stay here—not when he finds out I lied and my parents don't want me working for him after all.

I sniffled and felt those tears forming again. One dropped down my cheek and onto the spider's head. I better not ruin you, I thought, wiped my cheek and put the spider back in the trunk.

Then my mom's voice floated up. "Oh David, David, where could she be? What are we going to do?" And she began to cry.

I couldn't hear my father's reply. But I could tell he was comforting her.

Soon I heard a faint creak and a slam, and I knew they'd gone.

I felt real bad. Wait, wait, I wanted to yell. I'm here! Don't cry. But I couldn't. I couldn't go back and stand there while she yelled at me some more and told me how impossible I am. And besides, part of me was glad she was crying. At least it showed she missed me—even if she didn't care much about me when I was there. But the trouble was, I knew that wasn't true. She did care. But she had funny ways of showing it. She always wanted me to be a certain kind of kid—maybe the kind she was. She once told me that her favorite thing when she was a girl was writing in her diary and playing school. She wasn't the kind of kid who liked scientific experiments or finding out what makes things work or tarantulas. So how could she ever understand me? Then all the tears I'd been holding back burst out. I cried and cried and cried. I cried for me, for Ariadne, for everything. And I cursed Julie Lindstrom, who got me into this mess. I stopped crying, lay down on the cot and cried some more. I bawled so loud the pigeons on the roof probably got scared and flew away. After a while I fell asleep.

I knew I must've slept for a long time, because when I woke up the clouds were gone and the sun was pouring through the little window. I went downstairs, and sure enough, it was noon. I locked the front door and decided to feed the animals early today and then feed myself. I really didn't want to go back up into the attic—to tell you the truth it was getting me kind of depressed—but I knew it wasn't safe for me to stay downstairs, so back up I went. I didn't

158

feel like reading any more magic books, so I decided to write my paper for Ms. Eggleston—in case I ever went back to school. Or maybe I could send it to her in the mail just so she'd know I'm not so dumb after all.

"This poem," I wrote, "is about a snake—the narrow fellow in the grass. I don't know what kind of snake, but I guess it doesn't matter in this poem. The writer, Emily Dickinson, talks about how snakes move and where they like to sleep and stuff and what they look like. I think by whip lash she means a whip and not the thing that happens to your neck when you're in a car accident. A snake sort of looks like a whip. Anyway, this writer is afraid of snakes. They make her cold and scared. Zero at the bone. I like the poem even though I like snakes and I'm not scared of them, because the writer told her true feelings and also looked at snakes real close to describe them. I think she likes snakes more than she thinks she does."

When I finished, I read it over and I was pretty pleased. I wished I could write about Buster's poem too, but I still wasn't sure I understood it.

Palette

In summer I walk on diamond dust
Amidst Kandinsky blues.
In winter I flake off railing rust
And pour sand out of my shoes.

What did it mean? I could ask Mom who Kandinsky is, I thought. Then I remembered Mom wasn't there.

The rest of the afternoon passed pretty slowly. I read some more and ate some more and did one hundred jumping jacks, which surprised me because I never liked doing them in gym. And I looked out the window a lot. It was going to be suppertime soon. And nighttime. And it would be Tuesday and Markham and Lucy would come back and what was I going to do? I bit my lip. I was afraid I was going to cry again, and I was just as tired of crying as I was of staying in the attic. And then the door opened and Buster stepped into the room.

He was dressed in regular clothes—just like he'd been once before. I should've been surprised to see him, but somehow I wasn't. He didn't seem surprised to see me either. "You found me," I said.

"I found you," he answered, sitting down next to me on the cot.

"Did my parents call you and tell you I was missing?"

"No and no. Tessa told me when I came by to pick her—and you—up so you could get your spider."

From the way he said it, I knew Tessa and I hadn't fooled him, that he knew all along Ariadne was going to be my spider. "Did you tell my parents you knew where I was?"

"No. I don't believe in telling on people. . . . But

I do believe that telling the truth, laying your cards on the table, not pulling your punches, giving it to 'em straight, however and with whatever cliché you want to put it, is, in the long run, the best way of doing things."

"I haven't been very honest lately, have I? I guess you can go ahead and hate me just like everyone else does."

Then he did surprise me. He kissed me gently on the forehead. "No one could ever hate you, Gloriana."

And I started to cry. "Oh, B . . . Buster . . . wh . . . what . . . am I . . . going to do? I'm . . . re . . . really in a . . . m . . . mess . . ." I blubbered.

Buster didn't say anything, just pulled out a big red bandanna and handed it to me. I cried some more and blew my nose and wiped my eyes.

Finally, Buster said, "Want to tell it to me from the beginning?"

"Didn't Tessa tell you?" I said dully.

"I'd rather hear it from you."

So I told him.

"Well," he said when I'd finished, "that's certainly quite a good story."

"Now you know why I can't go home ever again . . . except I can't stay here either. . . . Hey, maybe . . . Could I maybe . . . do you have . . . er . . . any room in your house?"

He smiled. "I'm very flattered that you'd like to move in with me, but I'm afraid, a) I live in a small apartment and not a house; b) I make a terrible roommate. . . . Gloriana, would you like my advice?"

I nodded.

"Go home and tell your parents the whole story. You may be surprised at how they behave. Look at it as an experiment in psychology: How do parents act when their kid tells them the truth?"

"I already know how they'll act."

"Tsk, tsk, Gloriana. I'm surprised at you. That's a very unscientific attitude."

I smiled a little smile. "I guess you're right," I finally said. "Okay. I guess I might as well go home."

"Want me to go with you?"

"No. I might as well face them alone." I picked up my knapsack and started for the door. Then I turned. "Hey, Buster, can I ask you a question?"

"Shoot."

"Who is Kandinsky?"

Buster smiled. "He was a painter who painted the richest, most beautiful colors you can imagine. Colors that make you so happy you want to sing."

I thought a minute and said, "Can I ask you one more question? Do you ever think about how much better things were when you were a kid?"

"Why, Gloriana, you understand my poem!"

"I do? Oh, I do!"

"Except they're really not so nice and simple when you're a kid either, are they? Maybe they're never really nice and simple for folks like us."

We looked at each other and smiled. And right then I felt that if I were ten years older and liked boys I'd ask Buster to marry me on the spot. And I thought that he might even accept.

23

Buster was half right. I was half surprised at the way my parents behaved. When I walked in, they were sitting in the kitchen with Rona, Tessa and Ms. Eggleston. "Lizzie!" "You're home!" "Are you all right?" "Where were you?" Everybody seemed to be talking at once. I looked at Tessa and couldn't tell if she was relieved or angry or both. "Oh, Lizzie" was all she said.

"Well, where were you?" Mom said. I could tell she was trying to control her temper because there were other people there.

"In Markham's attic," I said quietly.

"In where?" My mother's voice rose. "But we went to his house and looked all over. Didn't you hear us?"

"Nora," my dad warned.

"Well, Lizzie. You certainly gave us all a fright," Ms. Eggleston said. "Your parents called me and asked if you had by any chance turned up in class. I know you had a report due today, but I told them I didn't think you'd cut class to avoid handing it in." She smiled.

"I'm sorry I cut, Ms. Eggleston," I said. "And I did do the report." I fished it out of my knapsack. "I was going to write a second one on another poem too, but I only just figured out what the poem means."

Ms. Eggleston looked a little surprised, but she smiled again and took my paper. "Well, I must say that was very diligent of you. I'll read it tonight. And now, I'm sure you have things to discuss with your parents, so I'll leave you. . . . Don't bother to get up—I can find my way out." And she left.

"I'd better be going too," said Tessa. "My mother is stationed by the phone in case *you* call."

I excused myself and walked her to the door. "Buster found me," I said. "He's the one who told me about the attic."

"Oh, Lizzie," Tessa said again.

"Are you mad at me?"

"Yes. No. I don't know. I guess we both blew it."

"I guess we did. . . . I'll call you later. If they let me use the phone."

She nodded and went.

I walked slowly back into the kitchen.

"Rona," Dad was saying, "don't you have something else to do?"

"No," Rona said with a little smirk. "I want to stay here for the fireworks."

"Rona!" Mom said sharply.

Uh-oh, I thought. Here we go. "Let her stay." I sighed. "It doesn't matter anyway."

"What do you mean, 'It doesn't matter anyway'?" Mom snapped.

"Nora, please," Dad said. "Lizzie, your mom and I and your sister too have been—and are—very upset. Please understand that. But I think we have to understand something too and that is what made you so unhappy you ran away."

So I took a deep breath and told them. I told them that I hated school—except science—and all those dancing classes they made me take and being funny-looking and not being pretty like Rona or smart and pretty like Tessa. I told them how I tried to tell them what I did like but they didn't listen. I told them how much I wanted a pet tarantula and that nobody seemed to want me to have any kind of pet at all, much less a spider. I told them how I tried to raise the money to get Ariadne and how it all backfired. I couldn't stop talking. It was like a dam had burst or something. And all the time I talked, Dad listened and Rona chewed her nails and Mom looked like her dam was about to burst, which it almost did when I told about selling her ring at the flea market.

"What? You did what? My ring! My diamond ring!" she yelled.

But Dad patted her arm and told her we'd figure out what to do about that later.

Finally, I finished talking and sat there, exhausted.

"Wow!" Rona said.

"You can say that again," said Dad.

But Mom said in a harsh voice, "If you expect me to be impressed with this, I can tell you I'm not. Lying! Running away from home! Selling my ring!"

"Oh, Nora," Dad said. "I have the strongest desire to tell you to go to your room."

"Don't worry. You don't have to tell me. I'm going there before I commit child abuse!" And she stomped out.

There was a long silence. And that's when Dad surprised me. He said, "I wish you had told us this before . . . before this mess happened. I wish your mother and I had made you feel you could have told us."

And Rona mumbled something about being sorry she was mean sometimes too.

"Are you going to punish me?" I said.

Dad smiled sadly. "I think you've punished yourself enough, don't you?"

I didn't understand exactly what he meant, so I just said, "Mom will never forgive me."

"Oh yes she will."

"No she won't. She hates me."

"Oh, Lizzie," Dad said. "No one hates you, least of all your mom. But I think she can't quite make sense out of this person she gave birth to. Look, why don't you wash your face and pay a visit to Tessa, and I'll go talk to your mom."

"Okay," I said, getting up and going over to the sink. I almost never wash up at the kitchen sink, but I didn't feel like going to the bathroom. I turned on the tap, reached for the soap and then noticed something strange. The soap was sitting in the soap dish. Now this dish has two parts—it's like a little plate with holes in it to let the soap drain down into the bottom part, which is like a cup. Usually it sat nice and snug on the bottom part, like this:

But this time the plate part was slightly off. Like in the magic cylinder I read about when someone had pushed the spring to make a coin or a watch or a ring disappear.

I closed my eyes and picked up the soap and the top together.

"Lizzie, what are you doing?" Dad asked.

Then I held my breath, opened my eyes and looked into the bottom part. And there, resting in a little puddle of soapy water, was one bright, shiny, beautiful diamond ring.

24

Well, I could tell you Mom apologized and hugged me and told me I was the best daughter in the world and that we all piled into the car and went to Noah's and I bought my tarantula, but that's not the way it happened.

I went to Tessa's, on Dad's advice, and didn't even see Mom's face when he handed her the ring. I told Tessa everything that had happened. We were pretty quiet together until she decided she wasn't mad at me after all.

"But what a shame—all that work to get Ariadne and now it's too late," Tessa said.

"Please, I'd rather not talk about it. It hurts too much," I said.

Tessa was silent a minute, and then she said, "Okay.

Let's talk about Julie Lindstrom instead and what we're going to do to her." Her eyes had a wicked gleam in them and that made me grin.

"Okay. Let's."

So we talked about cutting off her hair or tying her up and leaving her in the woods (except there aren't any around here) or making a voodoo doll of her to stick pins in ("That's not scientific," I said) until finally Tessa hit on the perfect plan. We would lure her to Markham's house with the promise of my job, get her to go up into the attic to meet the giant stuffed spider and lock her in. We only needed to work out a few details and Julie Lindstrom would get just what she deserved.

Then I went home and had dinner just with Dad and Rona. Mom had a screaming headache, Dad said, and couldn't come down, but she did tell Dad to thank me for finding her ring. I felt weird and depressed. I preferred Mom's yelling at me to the silent treatment. I washed the dishes and Rona dried. She was nicer to me than usual and asked if I had learned any neat tricks working for Markham. I felt pretty good about her, so I guess that's how I ended up telling her about Markham's sawing me in half and how it was done. She seemed real interested and asked me a lot of questions, which I answered. Afterward she went out to visit her friends and I went to my room. I was nearly asleep when Mom came in.

"Lizzie," she said softly.

"Ummm," I ummed.

She kissed my cheek, tucked the blanket around my neck and left. I wasn't sure whether or not I dreamed the whole thing. But it sure felt nice.

Julie was already at it when I got to school the next day. She was huddled in a corner of the classroom with a bunch of the other kids. The minute I saw them I knew they were talking about me.

Julie's voice rose above the group. "And I hear she ran away from home . . ."

"Yeah? Wow!" Sarah Leibel said.

"I bet Ms. Eggleston will flunk her," said Tommy Fredericks.

Then they saw me and stopped.

"Well, Lizzie, seen any good webs lately?" Julie said, and everyone else giggled.

I felt myself turn red. But I took a deep breath and thought about Tessa and my plans for Julie Lindstrom and felt a lot better.

And then Ms. Eggleston came in.

"Well, class, I've read your reports and I must say I was pretty pleased—with a few exceptions, of course."

"Guess who's one of the exceptions," Julie whispered loudly, glancing at me, and the class laughed.

Ms. Eggleston ignored her and handed back all the

papers except mine. "Lizzie," she said, "would you please see me at lunchtime?"

I frowned and nodded, and lowered my head, but out of the corner of my eye I could see Julie Lindstrom and she was smirking.

"You wanted to see me, Ms. Eggleston," I said when everyone else had gone to the cafeteria.

"Yes. It's about your paper. Will you give me a frank answer, Lizzie?"

I nodded.

"Did you really write this yourself?"

I stared at her. What kind of question was that? "Yes. Yes, I did," I said, confused.

Ms. Eggleston looked hard at me and said, "Yesterday you mentioned a second poem you liked. Can you recite it?"

"Yes," I said, and I did.

"Can you tell me what it means and why you like it?"

So I did that, and when I got to describing Buster and how he said he likes to astonish people, she smiled. "Oh, Lizzie. *You* astonish me. All year you've had me fooled. I thought you hated poetry and reading and 'stuff.' "

I got embarrassed, but I said, "I do hate them. Most of the time. But I like the two poems I told you about."

"Well, maybe there are some others you'd like too if you read them. In any event, I believe you did write this paper and I'm going to give you an Excellent on it, plus extra credit for the second poem."

"Thanks, Ms. Eggleston!"

"Don't thank me," she said, just as she had once before to Julie Lindstrom. "You deserve it."

I almost yelled, "Yippee," as I ran to the cafeteria. And then I bumped right into Julie.

"Hey, watch where you're going. You almost made me spill my chocolate pudding. But I suppose people who spend most of their time looking at spiders don't have any manners," Julie said.

And suddenly, something in me snapped. "And people who squeal on other people have less manners than that!" I said in a loud voice.

Julie didn't say anything. She just turned red.

"Ever since we've been in school together, Julie Lindstrom, you've made fun of me and tried to get everyone else to make fun of me too. And that was bad enough . . ."

"Oh boy," she interrupted, "Ms. Eggleston must have given you a pain."

"As a matter of fact, Ms. Eggleston gave me an E, plus extra credit. Here's my paper if you don't believe me!" I hollered. And I was sorry I did. The report wasn't important. I mean, it was, but it wasn't as important as what I wanted to say to Julie. So I said quickly, "It's you who give me a pain. You're a baby and a tattletale. All you do is whine and wheedle and talk behind people's backs. If it hadn't been for you, I could've gone on working for Markham the Magician and I could've bought my tarantula. But you went and told on me. Julie Lindstrom, you're nothing but a nasty, bigmouthed creep!"

And then something in Julie must've snapped, because she took her chocolate pudding and threw it at me. But her aim wasn't too good and it plopped on the floor instead.

"Fight! Fight!" yelled Sarah Leibel and Tommy Fredericks and some other kids. And someone stuck a pudding in my hand and bumped me. I lurched forward and the gooey stuff flew out of my hand and all over Julie's new pink dress.

And she went really crazy. She started running from table to table, grabbing chocolate puddings off kids' trays and throwing them at me and yelling, "I hate you, Lizzie Silver. I've always hated you. You do better in science than I do, people like you more than me, and now you even got an E from Ms. Eggleston."

I couldn't do anything but stare at her and duck.

The other kids were yelling and laughing, and pretty soon they started picking up puddings and heaving them around the room.

Julie didn't even notice them. And she also didn't notice Mr. Jackson running into the cafeteria—where

he was supposed to have been on duty all along and wasn't—followed by a red-faced Ms. Martinez. Julie just grabbed her tenth dish of pudding and yelled at the top of her lungs, "And furthermore, I hate you because you're taller than me!"

It was such a weird thing to say, the other kids kind of froze, like in a film. And then Julie pitched the pudding and it landed with a dull squish on Mr. Jackson's tie. Mr. Jackson looked stunned, but not as stunned as Julie. There she was, neat, proper Julie Lindstrom, with her hands and face and dress all smeared with chocolate pudding. Her eyes got big and she raised one hand to her mouth and let out a little cry. And Mr. Pincus, the principal, walked in.

"Good grief," he yelled. "What is this, a Laurel and Hardy movie?"

Nobody said a word.

"Who started this?" Mr. Pincus asked.

"Uh . . . um . . ." Mr. Jackson stammered. "I believe . . . this one." He pointed to Julie.

"You believe? Weren't you here on duty?"

"Uh . . . um," Mr. Jackson stammered again. Then he said in a shocked voice, "She threw a pudding at me."

"And what was the reason for such behavior?" Mr. Pincus asked Julie.

But Julie just whimpered.

I didn't want to say anything, but I knew it was

all going to come out anyway, so I said, "Mr. Pincus, she was trying to hit *me* with the pudding. We were having an argument."

"I see," said Mr. Pincus. "Both of you come down to my office where we can discuss this matter further. And as for the rest of you," he said to the other kids, "get some paper towels and clean up this mess."

When we got out into the hall, there was Tessa. She was late for lunch because she'd been rehearsing turning the pages of the piano for Ms. Whelpley for the graduation exercises. Tessa stared at Mr. Pincus, and Mr. Jackson with the chocolate pudding on his tie, and Julie who looked like she wanted to curl up and die, and me. "Wow!" was all she said. I looked back at her. I knew I should've been scared because there I was going to the principal's office for fighting in the cafeteria, but all I could do was grin because there wasn't any more reason to lure Julie Lindstrom to Markham's house and lock her in the attic with the giant spider. There wasn't any reason to get back at her anymore, because she had done it for me. Julie Lindstrom had made a fool of herself, and that was the worst punishment she could ever have.

25

Well, maybe you thought that was the end of the story—that I got back at Julie and got punished and I learned never to lie or be sneaky again. Or maybe you thought it would be years later and the ugly duckling would have turned into a swan. Or maybe, like my mother, you'd have thought that by now I'd have outgrown my love for spiders. If that's what you thought, you're wrong! Because I'm still the same ugly duckling who loves spiders just the way I did before, even though I never did get my Ariadne, which makes me very sad. But all the stuff I went through wasn't a total waste, because now I'm about to be a star.

You see, after the chocolate pudding fight, Mom picked me up at school. I thought she was really going to let me have it, but she fooled me—I mean, she did bawl me out a little, but she looked like she was going to laugh the whole time she was doing it. And she told me about how when she was a kid there was this nasty girl named Jeannine Hertzfeld who used to tell everyone Mom wore dirty underwear and things like that. Mom got back at her by painting a mustache and a beard on a picture of a ballerina Jeannine had done and was especially proud of. Well, after we finished laughing, Mom surprised me even more by saying I could keep my job because Markham had called her and said I was "invaluable" and he felt the experience was "educational and good for developing a sense of responsibility" for me.

"Markham said that?" I asked.

"Well, not in those exact words," said my mother. "And now you'd better get to work."

And that's where the star bit comes in. When the whole class found out from Tattletale Julie about my working for Markham and having appeared in his act one day, they all wanted to see him and me perform. So Ms. Eggleston, of all people, asked me if I'd be willing to be a magician's assistant just one more time. I said I'd think about it, but I didn't have to think too long because I really wanted to do it, if Markham said yes, and that's what I told Ms. Eggleston. She called up Markham and he said he'd be delighted.

So here I am once more waiting in the wings. I'm a nervous wreck. The Magic Lantern is packed. Out in the audience are Mom and Dad and Rona and Tessa and Mr. and Ms. Lawrence and Ms. Eggleston and my whole class (except for Julie Lindstrom, whose parents have grounded her for the rest of June). Markham and I are going to do a surprise illusion called "The Spider and the Lady." It's an old trick and a complicated one. Markham, Lucy, Buster, Tessa and me had to work all week on building it. But it looks perfect. You can't tell where the mirror is at all. In fact, everything would be perfect if only I could have gotten Ariadne.

Now it's time. The curtain closes and Buster, Virginia and I push the illusion into place and I hear Markham begin the story of Mr. Boniface, a rich man who shut himself away in his big fancy house to study magic. "At first his friends tried to visit him," says Markham, "but soon they gave up because Mr. Boniface would not let them in. He just kept studying his book of spells. The weeds grew high around his house. The lamps grew dark. And across the front steps a gigantic spider spun a web."

Then Markham pauses and the curtains open and there is the big fancy house with the spiderweb across the steps. In the center of the web is a gigantic spider.

The audience screams.

"Finally one day," continues Markham, "Mr. Boniface ceased his studying. He realized he was lonely and wanted someone to talk to. He decided to visit some of his friends. But he did not get very far."

Slowly, the door at the top of the steps opens and Buster, in an old-fashioned frock coat and high collar, starts to descend. Then he sees the spider and stops.

"When he saw the spider," Markham says, "he had an idea. An idea of how to make the spider talk, of how to make it a companion, using magic."

Buster goes back through the door.

"So he set to work and prepared a great spell," Markham continues. "It took him a fortnight. But at last it was ready. He dressed in his magician's robes, put on his magician's hat and stood at the top of the stairs."

Buster reappears in a gorgeous blue-and-silver robe and hat.

The audience gasps a little.

"And then he spoke," says Markham.

"Amalada. Badalada. Falalala," chants Buster.

And smoke begins to pour across the stage, blotting out the spider and the web.

"Go, Lizzie," Virginia says.

I nod and get into place.

"Maladala. Kaladala. Baroom!" Buster roars.

And then a wind comes up and blows the smoke away and the audience goes wild.

For there, in the center of the web is the spider. Only instead of the spider's head, there is mine.

"It's Lizzie! Lizzie!" Sarah Leibel yells.

"How'd he do that?" asks Tommy Fredericks.

"I will tell you all the secrets of the universe. I am your companion for life," I say in a sinister voice.

"Wow!" is all Rona says.

And the curtain closes.

I get out of where I am and run to Buster. We hug. "You were wonderful!" we tell each other.

"I'm so glad I asked Markham what that spider in the attic was for and he was able to remember that his father had done an illusion with it that he found in an old book," I say.

"I'm glad you did too, Gloriana."

"Oh, that was terrific," Virginia says coming over to me. "And Buster, how splendid you look." I notice she is looking at him in a brand-new way—the way she used to look at Markham.

But the trick isn't over. Markham has stepped in front of the curtain and I hear him say, "But Mr. Boniface soon grew tired of his spider girl. She talked too much and she didn't always have her facts straight."

Everyone laughs, but I am confused. This isn't part of the trick we rehearsed. "Buster, what's happening?" I ask.

"Listen," he answers.

"So he decided to turn the creature back into a spider," Markham says.

I peek around the curtain. And suddenly, from the

flies—that's the ceiling of a stage—the giant spider drops down on a string and the audience really shrieks. Markham unhooks the spider as Lucy comes out from the other side pushing a big box. Markham opens it to show the audience that it's empty. He puts the giant spider inside. "But Mr. Boniface found this spider a little hard to manage, so he decided to practice the new shrinking spell he'd learned." Markham closes the box and spins it around. Buster speaks from off-stage, "Babala. Swabala!" And with a flourish Markham opens the box. The audience applauds, but I can't see what is inside.

"Assistant!" Markham yells, and Buster gives me a nudge. I run out in my red-satin leotard. Markham lifts out of the box a small glass bowl and there, in the center, is a black-and-orange tarantula.

"Ariadne," I whisper. "Oh, Ariadne, is it really you?"

Markham puts the bowl in my hands. "And they all lived happily ever after!" he says to the audience. "It's for you, Lizzie," he whispers. "It was Buster's idea for the best assistant I've ever had."

While the audience stamps and cheers, I grin and cry at the same time and think about how much I like happy endings.